EMILY
&
HERMAN

EMILY

&

HERMAN

A LITERARY ROMANCE

JOHN J. HEALEY

ARCADE PUBLISHING
NEW YORK

Arcade Publishing books may be purchased in bulk at special discounts for sales promotion, corporate gifts, fund-raising, or educational purposes. Special editions can also be created to specifications. For details, contact the Special Sales Department, Arcade Publishing, 307 West 36th Street, 11th Floor, New York, NY 10018 or arcade@ skyhorsepublishing.com.

Arcade Publishing® is a registered trademark of Skyhorse Publishing, Inc.®, a Delaware corporation.

Visit our website at www.arcadepub.com.

10 9 8 7 6 5 4 3 2 1

Library of Congress Cataloging-in-Publication Data

Healey, John J.
  Emily & Herman : a literary romance / John J. Healey.
     pages cm
  ISBN 978-1-61145-830-5 (alk. paper)
  1.   Dickinson, Emily, 1830-1886--Relations with men--Fiction. 2. Melville, Herman, 1819-1891--Relations with women--Biography. 3. Authors, American--19th century--Fiction. I. Title. II. Title: Emily and Herman.
  PS3608.E2355E45 2013
  813'.6--dc23

                                        2012046338

Printed in the United States of America

For Sole

Preface

I DISCOVERED THE MANUSCRIPT THAT FOLLOWS HERE *Emily &*
Herman in the early summer of 2011. It was jammed into a
cardboard banker's box, number twenty of twenty-two, containing a life's assortment of notes, syllabi, and even a collec-
tion of unpublished short stories pertaining to my grandfather,
Vincent P. Healey, Professor Emeritus of English Literature at
Amherst College. He died that spring.

I was his only grandchild and his house near Lenox, Massachusetts was left to me in his will. The two-story Cape Cod
dwelling, originally built in 1796, sits near the Stockbridge
Bowl less than a mile from where Nathaniel Hawthorne had
lived for a time, a time depicted in *Emily & Herman*.

My grandfather's area of expertise was American Renaissance literature. His book *The Epoch of Melville and Whitman* is
in its twelfth edition and is still read by graduate students at
many prestigious universities around the country. Some of
his personal library was left to Amherst, the rest remained
on the shelves in his study, including the beautiful edition of
Stevenson's *A Child's Garden of Verses* he had often read to me
when I was a boy.

Some of the boxes were damaged by mildew and bur-
rowing chipmunks. They were stored in the garage behind
his well-maintained 1945 Willys MB Jeep. It took me over a
month to sort through them all and for a time I toyed with
the idea of trying to interest Amherst in publishing his short
stories. But then I found *Emily & Herman*, a work he did not
write, but for which he had written the prologue (see page ix).

None of his friends and colleagues I spoke with knew anything about it, but all of them who have had the opportunity to read it agree upon its singular charm. One of those friends was a publisher, the publisher of the book you now hold in your hands (or that you are looking at on an eBook screen).

Why my grandfather never attempted to have it published remains a mystery. Perhaps he worried the academic world he lived in would react with ridicule. Perhaps he was simply too busy—the dedication he brought to his tutorials and to his students was legendary. We might even consider the possibility that he wrote it himself, penning the preface as a witty ruse. Whatever the reason I think he would have been very pleased by this edition.

J. J. Healey
Lenox, Massachusetts 2012

Prologue

THE FOUND MANUSCRIPT IS A LITERARY DEVICE EMPLOYED most famously perhaps by Miguel de Cervantes Saavedra in *Don Quixote de la Mancha*. In the case I lay before you, it is not a stratagem at all but merely the simple truth, for I did find this manuscript, *Emily & Herman*, typed and rife with penned-in corrections, ten years after its author departed this earth. The romantic account contained within it, in which four iconic figures of American letters—Walt Whitman, Nathaniel Hawthorne, Herman Melville, and Emily Dickinson—play leading roles, is a work of fiction. For the reader who might have difficulty loosening ties to what she or he believes to have been the reality of these writers' lives, I suggest the following considerations:

The period in which this tale unfolds, the summer of 1851, was not chosen arbitrarily. In 1851, Walt Whitman was thirty-two years old, a Jack-of-all-trades, and master of none. The work for which he will always be remembered had yet to be put on paper.

In 1851, Nathaniel Hawthorne, the senior member of the foursome, was an established author. It might even be said his best work was already behind him. As depicted in this tale, he really was a friend to his Berkshire neighbor, Herman Melville. Over that summer they lived a carriage ride apart and saw each other frequently. Although Hawthorne had the highest regard for Melville's prose, it was not without ambivalence. Like Salieri with Mozart, the esteem Hawthorne held for his friend was an oleo of love and fear, admiration and envy. He, more than anyone, was fully aware of the depth and majesty contained within the work Melville slaved at that year and that was dedicated to Hawthorne upon its completion—for in the summer of 1851, Herman Melville was finishing *Moby-Dick*.

Melville, a true aristocrat, and already known as the author of semi-autobiographical sea yarns, was composing a work many consider to be the Great American novel of all time. His days before the mast were over. He had married and lived between Manhattan and the countryside of Western Massachusetts hemmed in by mountains and forests, surrounded by willful women. A disaster in all matters financial, he owed money to virtually everyone and was in desperate need of fresh literary success. He hoped and believed *Moby-Dick* would give it to him.

Emily Dickinson was barely twenty in 1851. She had written very little and had never published. Though unusually sensitive, she was a vibrant and engaging young woman that summer, years away from being cosseted by phobias and crippled by irrational fears. The image most readers have of Emily Dickinson today is of an older Emily, a deeper Emily perhaps, but also a tragic Emily who, as those she loved died around her, reduced her universe to the four walls of her room in Amherst. The story you are about to read thus, takes place in a time before any of that came to pass.

The author, who chose to remain anonymous and whose wishes I can only respect, lived for a time at the Emily Dickinson house during the period it served as an Amherst faculty residence. The following note was paper-clipped to the first page of the manuscript:

When Emily Dickinson died, in 1886, only eleven of her eighteen hundred poems had been published. Among the vast amount of documents she left behind were three unsent love letters, all of them addressed to: "Master." For decades, Dickinson scholars have been spinning theories concerning the identity of this person. The conceit of this novel, entirely fictitious, is that the "master" was Herman Melville.

For all we know, the delightful story told here actually happened. The degree of enchantment attained by its readers will depend on their personal taste and imagination. More to the point perhaps, is the expression an old professor of mine of Italian literature, a man who came from a wise and more permissive culture, would often say, 'Se non e vero e ben trovato.' True or not, it is a fine story.

V. P. Healey
Amherst, 1965

1

MIDSUMMER. MIDMORNING. PLACID, FRESH AIR. WOOD smells and the smell of drying hay, and a scent of withering lilac blossoms drifting through the barn's open window. Out that window is Greylock Mountain. During the winter and covered with snow it had emulated the leviathan but now it rested massive and ponderous in a verdant haze. Leaning forward, pen in hand, about to revise the day's final sentence, he listened to bees going about their work outside.

At it since seven and having decided how to end his tale, he determined to reward himself with a break. He rose from his chair and approached the washstand, eyeing a dining needle stilled upon the white chipped sill. Scrubbing ink off of his fingers he glanced at his reflection in the looking glass. It may be raucous and ungainly, he thought, but it's getting done. He smiled at himself and was then embarrassed by how it made him look, so he turned away.

He drank a cup of water and put the pages aside for his sister Augusta to copy out. Using a piece of scrimshaw, he anchored them fast to the desktop that was stained from the doves roosting on the beams above. The table had belonged to his father's brother Thomas who had inherited it from his grandfather, the original Major Melville. It gave off a sweet attic aroma that evoked the past. He remembered how at his grandfather's house in Boston the piece had rested in an ornate dressing parlor under a painting of Pigeon Cove. On numerous occasions his father, inebriated and insisting on male conversation deep into the night, and finding his older son Gansevoort uncooperative, regaled him with tales of how the old Major had kept a mistress in that little coastal village just north of Rockport, a beautiful young widow whose husband had served under the Major's command in the Continental Army.

He dried his hands on a piece of sack cloth and looked out the window at the overgrown grass and lilac trees, at the piled bales, at one of the wagon horses rubbing against a tree. He thought of how all of them—the mistress, his father, his uncle, and grandfather, his older brother Ganesvoort, too—were gone and buried. All of that once-anxious and vibrant flesh had been transformed into darkened waste that had surely seeped through rotting pine by now fertilizing the surrounding loam. In his grandfather's time the family had status and money. The Major had taken part in the Boston Tea Party and commanded his regiment during the war with distinction. In his later years, Boston society considered him a character due to his stubborn persistence in wearing fashions redolent of his most vibrant years—breeches and frock, linen cravats and buckled pumps. Herman's father Alan, ashamed perhaps by the Major's eccentricities, spent long periods abroad, making a career in French dry goods while sampling the ladies who went with them before marrying and settling in Manhattan. After mentioning the widow of Pigeon Cove, Alan often would go on about a particular girl he himself had loved in Paris, wondering what had become of her, a wondering that inevitably altered his alcohol-induced sentimentality transforming it into a depressive quietude, while his young son worried his mother might be listening. All of them, Herman thought, had come from and returned to "dust." And yet there he was, still alive and spry enough, a striving scrivener confined in this country house his father-in-law had paid for, filled with women, nary a sail or a harpoon within a hundred miles.

He set out to find Elizabeth, his wife, seven months pregnant with their second child. When he left her in bed that morning, rising to work at dawn, she had been "out of sorts" once again. He came into the main house and saluted his mother and sister Helen and almost tripped over his son Malcolm, sound asleep on a quilted throw rug by the hearth. The monstrous brown Newfoundland dog lay next to the dark-haired boy and it raised its tail to let him know all was well. Climbing upstairs and entering the bedroom, he found Elizabeth on her back with the shades drawn, one hand resting upon her swollen womb, the other holding a damp cloth over her eyes aflame with allergies.

"Is that you?"

"Aye."

"And Barney?"

"Dreaming like an angel by the hearth."

"I trust there is not a fire lit."

3

"Just ashes from last night and mother is reading not five feet from him."

He sat beside her.

"Can I get you anything?"

"No."

It was clear she preferred to remain undisturbed. He studied her wrist and remembered it belonging to a lively young girl from Boston.

"I'm finished for the day."

"That's a good thing then. Perhaps you can devote more time to us now." The tone was accusatory, but he did not take it to heart.

"I'm going to take a few days off and bring what I have down to the printer next week."

He had hoped for a kiss, or a conspiratorial smile, the kind she used to offer when he spoke with her about his work. He patted her knee and then stood up again, hoping it was the pregnancy and the discomforts the season always brought that was putting her so at odds.

An hour later he was carrying the boy in his arms along the path to the lake. The dog, pleased by the unexpected change in the morning's routine, loped ahead, crisscrossing, snout close to the ground. The comely Irish cleaning girl's arrival to their room had proven an instant cure for Lizzie's malaise. When he bid them adieu both women were taking over the kitchen, planning the midday repast and catching up on local gossip.

He hoped the new child would be a girl, for something told him that might help soothe things between them. Even more he hoped The Whale book would be a success. Such an outcome, more than anything else, would throw them a lifeline. The monies owed to Brewster and Stewart, to his father-in-law, and to Harpers cut into him like shark teeth.

"Would you care for a little sister Barney?"

The boy, who weighed little more than a September Blue-fish, turned to look at him, leaning his head back, ignorant of the meaning behind the sounds emanating from his father's lips. He transferred the boy from one side to the other and began to hum him a sea ditty while mentally reviewing his last meeting with Hawthorne. He was still feeling sheepish from the excess of enthusiasm that had possessed him when they had last conversed through the night. At first he blamed it on the brandy. But in his heart he knew it had been a reaction to Nathaniel's comparative reticence. If his friend were a looser, freer soul it would be easier to interact with him in a more measured manner. But the man's solemnity and verbal stinginess, especially pronounced that night, had transformed Melville into a pup too eager for praise and petting. He vowed to keep his compensatory instincts at bay and, in the future, to match the man with doses of his own medicine.

A snowshoe hare appeared, emerging from a stand of beech. It stopped to sniff the sir and then dashed across the path before them, disappearing into the safety of some tall grass. The dog, too far ahead, barely had time to notice.

At the lake's edge, it gladdened him to see there was not another soul about. He stripped down and removed the diaper and chemise from his son, folding everything over the bough of a nearby pine. Lifting the boy up once again he walked into the water. The sandy, clayish bed was slippery with patches of slithering grass. The lake was warm on the surface and cold beneath. The dog barked in protest, running back and forth along the narrow shore before venturing in as well, suddenly quiet, all energies bent upon staying afloat while it did its best to remain close to the man and boy who continued to swim farther out.

Melville was impressed by the boy's equanimity. His small face displayed a countenance of agitated delight mixed with what could only be described as pleasurable caution. Being a father, fatherliness, overwhelmed Melville at times, feeling one minute in concord with and entranced by the office, linked in turn to his own sire for whom he had felt such affection, only to feel when the tide shifted, entrapped and inadequate.

The irony of this inland life was especially pungent that morning. The sailor and adventurer, the ocean swimmer at ease in Atlantic and Pacific swells, on intimate terms with a multitude of Polynesian atolls, the whaling man on the verge of completing a woman—and childless yarn of biblical length that took place on the highest of seas—confined now to this valley that was laced with his family history, its lovely but trivial lake, deep in New England and far from any ocean air. Instead of dolphins and orcas and sperm whales to swim amongst, there were only sun perch and snapping turtles. God forbid I should cramp and drown in such a place and go down in the annals of literature a comical footnote. Herman Melville, author, the man who lived with cannibals, drowns from a leg cramp in Melville Lake.

But he was a strong swimmer, something a surprising number of his fellow crewmen had not been, and he swam about enjoying the exercise to his limbs, holding his son aloft the way the naked maidens of Nukuheva had held their sarongs above their heads while swimming out to the ships. He swam that way a good ten minutes before returning to where he could stand. The dog, looking more like a small wet bear, made its way back to the shore and shook three or four times before, exhausted and relieved, it sat upon its haunches.

He felt considerably more exposed leaving the water than he had going in and he made haste to dry himself with his shirt before pulling on his trousers. Then he reclined upon a patch of grass under a tree with the boy and the dog in shade-speckled sunlight. The dog hunkered down to chew on a dry pinecone and the boy, naked and relaxed, lay on his back looking up through branches.

He was at home here. More so perhaps than he had been at sea or in Albany or in Boston. Melvilles had been coming here, especially during the summer months, for decades. It had been wise to return here. The streets of lower Manhattan first and foremost and then these fields and ponds irrigated with clear Berkshire air were home. He thought back on the summers he had missed here when he was twelve and already working at the State Bank in Albany, living at his uncle Peter Gansevoort's mansion while his widowed mother and his brothers and sisters had all frolicked at this lake with their cousins, fleeing the cholera. And now he was a grown man, married and a father himself, returned from his seafaring, back to his roots.

And he recalled how he had awakened that dawn in the grip of what had been a compelling and now forgotten dream. He had at first been unable to establish where or even who he was. The disorientation had only lasted a few seconds but it left him pensive and aware of being alive and mortal in a keener manner than usual. Leaning upon the earth there now, refreshed and seemingly content, watching the lake under a clear noon summer sun, his son cooing beside him and the dog now resting its massive head upon its front paws, the feeling returned. He wondered if it might be a first sign of age or some reaction to the impending completion of the book, some puritanical manifestation, a self-inflicted punishment for having felt so at ease that day. And as an exercise in orientation, if only to distract his mind from imagining how many heartbeats were left to him upon the Earth, he began to chart his position. He saw the lake from above, from a gull's perspective, and the path that linked it to his property where his wife and the new still-forming child and the comely young maid and his mother and sisters and all of his papers and books and possessions were. Rising higher he saw Lenox where Hawthorne lived. Rising higher still he could see the Connecticut River severing Massachusetts in half, and Boston and the Cape and, out at sea, Nantucket, where The Whale book began, and looking south, Long Island, and then the island of Manhattan, where he was born and where his younger brother Alan junior and his bride were breathing that very minute. Rising higher still he saw the vast country with oceans at either end, San Francisco where his brother Tom lived a sailor's life, and then across the vast Pacific seeing all of the tiny islands he had visited and known such wondrous people upon. It was, he knew, all there simultaneously, at that very moment, all of it, so far from each other according to one's choice of scale, each place and creature going about its business within each particular conscience's greedy and selfish present. "What," he asked himself, and it was a question he would sometimes pose aloud to intimates, "was more miraculous and mystifying than reality itself, ordinary, disheveled, run of the mill reality?"

The dog rolled over on its back with its front paws flipped down, completely at ease. The boy made gentle spitting noises, peeing upon himself. Herman resolved that during

his trip down to the city and back he would read a good
book or two from those he had brought back with him from
England. He had read Dante and Darwin simultaneously that
year, the blend of a sublime literature of antiquity with a
revolutionary modernity based on the careful observation
of simple animal life, the carapaces of turtles, the beaks of
birds. He felt blessed and invigorated to be living in such a
time when the most basic tenets of human belief and faith
were being challenged at their core and damn the clerics
who talked about him behind his back, the ones his mother
still tried to convince him to pray with. What better prayer
could there be than the untrammeled utterances coming
from his little boy's lips?

He reached the house sunburned and sweaty and he
handed the sleeping boy to Augusta, dressed in black as
always, who handed him a letter. He caught a glimpse of
Mary the maid who gave him a smile and a look that made
him conclude his appearance was that of a wild man. He
took the letter to his room where he refreshed himself and
changed for dinner. Then he broke the seal, recognizing the
careful script of Hawthorne.

My Dear Melville,

*Perhaps by the time your eyes peruse this most hastily composed
missive you will have impaled, slaughtered, and sold off your
massive albino cetacean! I do hope so for I have a proposal to
toss your way.*

He concluded his fears of having made an ass of himself
the other night were unfounded.

*There is a gentleman in Amherst well positioned in the
excellent college there I am beholden to visit in order to*

9

explore the possibility of departing classes in said institution and to thus avail myself of some income. I assure you this somewhat unorthodox manner of seeking remuneration has not originated in my brain! Tiz Sophia who is the culprit in this scheme and who has put the bayonet to my back. Whomever the imbecile was that deemed womanhood the meeker and fairer sex must have had a steel edge placed against him as well.

The long and the short of it is that I am setting out for Amherst this coming Sunday and it is my fervent desire to pay a call on you and Elizabeth to enlist you to accompany me on the rest of the journey. . . .

He read it aloud to Elizabeth, his mother, and sisters at dinner. As the peach cobbler was served, he wrote a rapid reply so that it might go out with that afternoon's post giving his neighbor time enough to make an alternate plan. They would of course be pleased to receive him at their home on his way east to Amherst, but Melville, in spite of his devotion to Hawthorne, had no desire to traipse around Massachusetts and had already made his plans to visit Manhattan.

2

My Dear Melville,

As I have informed you, no doubt on numerous occasions, my father and grandfather were sea captains who spent far more time riding swells than tending the hearth in Salem. If the yellow fever had not sent him to a saline grave some-where north of Surinam when I was just a lad, my father and namesake would surely have encouraged me to enter his realm of endeavor, as indeed I often dreamed about as a much younger and more fanciful fellow than I am at present. I risk repeating these observations to you because it occurs to me that one of the sources of our friendship, with respect to myself, is the life you have led—managing to combine a profession part of me always dreamed about but never had the gumption to pursue, in addition to your current life of letters. While I was wallowing through the dark and sorrowful homes, spirits, and copses of Salem in my Scarlet Letter, there you were spinning yarns describing the sensual and sinful nether regions of God's splendid orb! And now I learn you are close to finishing "The Whale"—for which you have my and Sophia's heartiest congratulations.

So I say unto you, nay, I order you as your superior officer (in years at least!), to embark upon this journey with me. Let us have our voyage together, be it only upon land, while time, so fickle and unpredictable, permits! I should mention that Sophia and I are looking to move. My Tappan landlords have insulted me of late and I do not think I could bear another summer in the Berkshires. With our newest child Rose just two months old the house has become a glorified nursery, something you too will have the pleasure of navigating once dear Lizzie comes to term this autumn! I, who have never ventured onto the sea, now feel a need to at least live aside it once again. Perhaps your present contentment in these hilly woods has something to do with an opposing set of circumstances. Be that as it may—this could very well be the last time we shall be living in such proximity to each other.

So let me repeat my bid and up the ante! Come with me to Amherst and afterward, posthaste, I shall accompany you to the Isle of Manna-Hata where I too have some overdue publishing business I should attend to. . .

Nathaniel Hawthorne, forty-seven years of age, still very handsome and as always wearing a Westcott and cravat, finished his letter upon the clean mahogany desk that had once belonged to Sophia's brother George. Having suffered the early humiliation of being left penniless and without an estate along with his mother and siblings after the untimely death of his father at sea, he made a point of always appearing respectable. As his publisher once said to him, 'You are a walking contradiction Hawthorne—the heart and pen of a relentless probing bohemian with the manner and dress of a *Bürgermeister*!'

He was an introspective and orderly man with a fertile imagination who lived an organized life in a neatly maintained household. The wooden floors of his rented red farmhouse were regularly scrubbed and waxed. Dogs were not admitted within. His daughter Una's cat was confined to the young lady's chamber. Though he and his young family struggled to survive, a maid was employed, full time, in order to ensure a general state of cleanliness. A stable hand worked part time tending the horses and the carriage and was charged with keeping the barn free of cobwebs, vermin, and manure. Hawthorne himself kept the garden free of weeds. He bathed in the Stockbridge Bowl each morning regardless of the weather and took long walks each afternoon mulling over his work.

He left his writing study and made his way to the main salon, keeping his head low so as not to bash it against the roof timbers. Sophia was there feeding little Rose. She faced the window, a white linen towel covering her naked breast. They exchanged greetings as he sat in the easy chair behind her to share the view of the mountains. Una and Julian ran about outside like wild beasts. He remembered the first time he had seen Sophia's breasts, in the darkness of their room at the Manse in Concord. The windows had been open and it smelled of all the rain that had fallen during that day—wet pine and wet grass and wet clothing. Girlish and slight and finely shaped they had only been available to him in the dark.

When he was finally permitted to touch them and to kiss them her shudders of pleasure surprised and alarmed them both. He wondered if she ever thought back to that first week they lived together almost nine years ago to the day.

"You realize you'll be gone for at least a week," she said, staring straight ahead.

Looking past her he could see a robin on the grass pulling a worm from the ground. He wondered if the worm felt anything and at the same time he passed judgment on the unappealing aspect of the robin. He had never shared in nor had he ever understood the lyrical regard assigned to them in poesy. To him they seemed a vulgar bird, lacking in subtlety and more akin to a member of a main street marching band.

"Will you miss me?" He asked her.

The back of her neck was still alluring. He would put his nose there at that very moment, would perch there listening to the suckling sounds of their new daughter had he any assurance she might allow him to.

"The question," she said, "is, will you miss me—me and the children? I somehow doubt it."

"That is a second question, posed before the first has been satisfied."

She looked at him as best she could over her shoulder.

"Of course I will miss you. I just wish you weren't so eager to go, I wish I were able to go with you, I wish we . . ."

Then he did go and plant his lips on the back of her neck.

"I wish it too. You'll be fine here. Your sister is good company. The blasted Tappans are at your beck and call. There is much to distract you."

"That there is."

"And I will miss you, you and the children. I will not lie and say the idea of wandering about on my own or talking into the night with our mad Melville or discussing work with my publisher does not call to me—I'm sure you too have moments when you would like nothing more than to be back in your room in Salem wondering what book to pick up next, what walk you might take with your sister, who might come to tea that afternoon."

"Never. But I do sometimes wish to be back with you at the Manse."

"I was just remembering our first days there."

"But now we are blessed with children."

"Blessed. And the primary reason for this trip has been at your urging remember."

"I know. Well it is tiresome, for the both of us, to live from month to month like this, year after year."

He took the baby's foot in his hand, smooth as a pebble in a rivulet, and then reached for the hand of his wife. Her skin smelled of cologne with a tinge of ambergris and it mixed with the odor of infant vomit that emanated from the linen towel. What did couples do at this point? Was there any way to maintain the initial entrancement without having to wait until the children were all grown and gone? What might such a regained state of marital solitude feel like then with so much gray shading the strands of one's hair? He thought with some chagrin that they would soon be on the move again—looking for yet another house—only a year and a bit after they had arrived there, overjoyed to finally have a place to themselves after almost five years of living with relatives. He truly could not grasp how Melville did it, constantly in sight of his mother and sisters. He recalled the verse he had copied out just as he and Sophia were settling in, written by Horace two score years before Christ was born, celebrating the Roman bard's relief at being sent off from Rome to live in the country—just as he had fled the vile streets of his native Salem.

> "I prayed for this: a modest swatch of land
> where I could garden, an ever-flowing spring
> close by, and a small patch of woods above
> the house. The gods gave all I asked and more.
> I pray for nothing more, but
> that these blessings last my life's full term."

On the day of his departure for Pittsfield and Amherst, fortune shone upon him. Sophia's friend Catherine Sedgwick came to visit and shared their dinner. While the coffee was being ground, Fanny Kemble, returned from Europe, suddenly arrived on her stunning black steed to offer Una and Julian a ride into the woods. In the midst of such social commotion and vibrant femininity, he took advantage and made his goodbyes correctly suspecting his "abandonment" of house and family would provide a pretext for extended commiseration by the time he had gone but a quarter of a mile.

Backing off from a cantor to a trot and breathing in the leaden, moist, late afternoon air he had come to abhor, he thought about the striking Fanny Kemble. She was an actress born in London into a family of thespians who had come to America where she fell in love with and married a rich admirer. Her dream had been to settle down and have children, and not long after that dream had been realized, she discovered to her horror that much of her spouse's fortune derived from plantations riddled with slaves who were treated abominably. The divorce their arguments about this issue led to had left her without support and without her two children. And so she had returned to the stage to earn her own living once more, and she kept a house, The Perch, near theirs—and of course she took great interest in Una and Julian, substitutes to help assuage her frustrated motherhood. He wondered what other frustrations might beset her. He wondered if she had a gentleman friend by now. He wondered at her offer made to him a week earlier, that they take her far roomier house rent free the following year, an offer he had been hesitant to share with Sophia. Best not to become too friendly with such a beautiful woman so capable and unattached. Discipline and denial in all things had served him well.

As his horse lifted its tail to drop an apple basket's fill of manure, they trotted past a tree from which a nest had fallen. He glanced down at it and perceived just enough to note that one of the chicks was dead and two others foundering. He wondered to what family of bird they belonged and what unfortunate turn of random events had brought about the nest's dislodgement.

He rode on in contemplation. What, in fact, could one do when faced with such a thing? The horse's hooves were surely trampling that very moment all manner of ants and beetles and crickets put in harm's path by the same inscrutable laws of chance. If he, a non-church-going, but still-believing Christian—and why not admit such a creed—could not bring himself to aide those much less fortunate who belonged to his own species and tribe, the beggars passed by so frequently in Boston and in New York, what in God's name was he obliged to do about such disasters fallen upon species that had been denied souls?

What was the verse, from Matthew? Ah yes . . .

Look at the birds of the air; they do not sow or reap or store away in barns, and yet your heavenly Father feeds them. Are you not much more valuable than they?

But logic dealt him another hand. The poetry of the New Testament was all well and good. These were not birds of the air, but fledglings, unable to yet take wing, who had fallen to the earth where no good would come to them. And he had seen them with his own eyes. Would he have passed an infant thus abandoned? And had not God created these creatures with a care very similar to that expended upon his own race that had been etched in God's image? What was the Christian thing to do? Where was the verifiable spiritual line between insect and bird, bird and animal, animal and man?

Though a good half a mile had been put between him and the broken nest, he found that the lugubrious thoughts he was apparently unable to shake were ruining an afternoon to which he had been looking forward with considerable enthusiasm.

"Damn it!" He cried aloud to the air, stopping his horse, and turning it about. At the very first, he felt immense relief, he felt younger, and was soon enjoying the boyish image of himself this rashly chosen mission of rescue was calling forth. But then he realized he had not the faintest notion what he was going to do. Would he guard them in his hat and transport them to Melville? Would he stop at the nearest farm and risk ridicule by asking a perfect stranger to care for such helpless creatures? Might his actual motive be the pleasure he would derive from telling this tale, putting himself in a gracious light? A dark taper rose within him from a place he was in no mood to elucidate urging him to put them, and him, out of their misery with two quick blows from the heel of his boot. Thus was his all too brief respite of recovered boyishness thrown into stormy seas and bandied about until he pulled up short some twenty paces from the tree.

Two cats had found the nest and were feasting. The chagrin he felt was of such intensity it robbed him of the energy required to chase them away. He just sat there in his saddle and watched them as they, in turn, measured his potential threat to them without ceasing their meal. Angry and feeling foolish he spurred his horse round yet again and resumed his journey.

3

'. . . my rebellious thoughts are many, and the friend I
love and trust in has much now to forgive. I wish I were
somebody else.'
(EXCERPT FROM A LETTER OF EMILY DICKINSON
TO A FRIEND, IN LATE 1850)

EDWARD AND EMILY NORCROSS DICKINSON WERE AWAY—
Edward on a train en route to New York City and Emily, his
wife, just arriving with their youngest daughter Lavinia for a
visit with the Norcross family in Monson. Relieved to have
their son Austin home from Boston they felt comfortable
leaving their middle child, Emily Elizabeth, in his company
there. Both siblings were supremely pleased to have some
respite from their dearly beloved "just ones" and to have
their cherished white clapboard manse on North Pleasant

Street to themselves. Austin, at this moment, was asleep in the downstairs parlor, *The Bride of Lammermoor* resting askew upon a chest gently rising and falling with the noiseless assurance of the twenty-two-year-old lungs respiring within. His sister Emily, two years his junior, soaked in the luxurious new bathtub their forward-looking and hygienically minded father had recently installed.

She inspected the small pink nubbly nipples upon her slight breasts, the perfect little "o" of her navel, the dark modest thatch of hair between her legs hiding a snug and oystery introitus. And she opined to herself that this is what women were. This is what they really looked like. So what was modesty? Men were muscular and hirsute with dangling things and women were curved and softer. None of the other animals, created each one by the same God Almighty as she, wore a strip of raiment and did not seem ashamed or any less noble for it. Little children were sometimes seen to run about undressed without exciting reprobation. And yet her clothing, worn each day since she could remember, covered virtually every bit of her, and were a button to be seen undone or the skirt of her dress inadvertently raised to show an ankle all manner of shame and disapproval would rain down upon her, not only from without but from within herself as well.

She expected the bestial strangeness of copulation had much to do with it. For men and women married to copulate. No one spoke about it as such but everyone thought about it. All of the clothing and liturgical admonishments and the solemn duty to be with child came down with a mighty focus on what one saw dogs up to in alleyways.

There she went, sinning again she was sure, just by entertaining such musings. But she could not resist. Resisting felt far stranger than looking straight and true. What went on within her head and heart was her own affair. It was only untoward and vulgar when spoken aloud or, worse still, actually engaged in! But what sort of Mighty God, fashioning creature after creature to live in abject naturality without a care in the world would then bestow upon His most beloved invention such strange restrictions and provisions for sin? She expected a bit of celestial humor at work.

Then, in a darker hue, she recalled Austin's doubts spoken to her just two evenings ago. They had been sitting on the porch after nightfall smelling the dampened summer pine, sipping currant wine, and counting fireflies.

"I see mankind marshaled in mighty hosts," he said, "yet under different banners, and marching on to the word of their several leaders, whom they believe, each his own, have received from the Omnipotent himself the true—and *only* true—chart of the route to knowledge, to happiness everlasting, and to him. And now *new* doubts encompass me, for if *either*, and only *one*, *which* is *right*?"

She thought him to be at his most handsome when struggling with such concerns, ones she shared with herself in private, and which she knew he had attempted to share with Susan Gilbert and her sister only to be faced with an icy wave of rejection.

"Go on," was all she said to him as she enjoyed the motion provided by the rocking chair she sat in that only her father could occupy when at home.

"I am besought on the one hand to join one standard and on the other, another—the advocates for the standard of the Cross appeal to me in the most solemn manner, as I value quiet from the gloomy doubts and fears within me—as I value perfect peace and happiness through a life eternal, in *God's* name to join them, for so surely as God is God, all the rest are marching on to death and perdition—but when I survey their ranks, and observe their comparative thinness, I hesitate. I ask myself, Is it possible that God, all powerful, all wise, all benevolent, as I must believe him, *could* have created all these millions upon millions of human souls, only to destroy them? That he *could* have revealed himself and his ways to a chosen few, and left the rest to grovel on in utter darkness? I *cannot* believe it. I can only bow and pray and hope that He teaches what He will—for my obedience shall be my highest pleasure."[1]

"Surely one can entertain such well-reasoned doubts without resorting to such anguish Austin."

"My anguish comes from the reaction such thoughts incite in Sue."

"Then, if you love her, in any case, perhaps a vow of silence regarding these matters might not be too hard a sacrifice."

He had laughed at that.

She pulled the plug of cork covering the drain and watched the water swirl away and when it was all gone she continued to lay there just a few moments more, her eyes closed in modesty, but enjoying the humid summer air wafting over her wet skin.

In the Garden of Eden neither Adam nor Eve had felt any shame about their nakedness—until Eve ate an apple from the forbidden Tree of Knowledge and offered it to her mate. For this simple act, they were banished and condemned to know disease and mortality, and made to feel the shame she felt then, and they were branded with original sin, the curse of

---

[1] Taken and adapted from a letter written by Austin Dickinson to Martha Gilbert in 1862.

which would be passed along to all their progeny. Surely this was just a story, a child's tale dreamt up long ago to explain the weight of woes besetting us.

Then there was the element of the serpent, an apt symbol to toss into the mix. She remembered Milton's line: ". . . Who first seduc'd them to that foul revolt? Th' infernal Serpent; he it was, whose guile Stird up with Envy and Revenge, deceiv'd The Mother of Mankind. . ." But why was it the serpent had tempted Eve and not her mate? Surely t'was a man that penned the tale.

She rose and reached for the linen towel and wrapped it about her and peered down to the yard in time to see two gentlemen dismounting by the picket fence. She did not recognize either one—friends of Austin's she presumed. The older of the two looked the proper squire, distinguished and self-satisfied. The other sat his horse better and had a more relaxed demeanor—perhaps tentative might be a better word. It was as if one of them had already fixed his compass while the other was still searching.

She dressed, returning to her natural unnatural state, and recalled the ending to Milton's poem she had memorized during her last year at Mount Holyoke.

> "In either hand the hastning Angel caught
> Our lingring Parents, and to th' Eastern Gate
> Led them direct, and down the Cliff as fast
> To the subjected Plaine; then disappeer'd.
>
> They looking back, all th' Eastern side beheld
> Of Paradise, so late their happie seat,
> Wav'd over by that flaming Brand, the Gate
> With dreadful Faces throng'd and fierie Armes:

Som natural tears they drop'd, but wip'd them soon; The World was all before them, where to choose Thir place of rest, and Providence thir guide: They hand in hand with wandring steps and slow, Through Eden took thir solitarie way."

4

Refreshed and dressed in white, she descended the stairs observing her brother Austin with the two riders now well inside their front hallway. Suddenly, all eyes turned upon her. Introductions were made—their surnames blazing into her like flaming arrows.

Knocking a riding crop against his boot, Hawthorne kept his gaze upon Austin Dickinson. "Clearly I should have written first. I don't know what possessed me not to do so?"

"But then we would never have had the pleasure of making your company," said Austin, smoothing back a lock of hair the way he did when he was agitated.

"I propose your lack of correspondence to be a telling detail," Emily said, looking at Hawthorne until he returned her gaze.

"And what might that be?"

"I believe it is known as ambivalence."

"About?"

"Why would a man of your literary standing feel the need to impart lessons to students who've read little more than the Bible and *The Pilgrim's Progress?*"

"Precisely for that reason I should think."

"Well put," she said, conceding with a blush.

"Might you have any notion as to how long your father will be in New York before proceeding on to Washington?" Melville asked, unknowingly irked by this flirtation.

"At least a fortnight. Of that I am certain," said Austin Dickinson.

"Well our next port of call is to be New York."—then, looking at Hawthorne—"Perhaps you can make Mr. Dickinson's acquaintance there."

"I will write to him straight away," said Austin, standing a bit taller.

"But perhaps we might all have some tea first," Emily said, still looking at Hawthorne.

"We've no intention of imposing upon you any more."

"Imposing?" questioned Emily. "I don't think so. Your appearance here has made our afternoon I should think, no Austin?"

"My sister is quite right. We insist you stay and rest a bit with us. We've the house to ourselves and know where all the better cakes are hidden."

Emily excused herself and put the kettle on the boil, gathered together cups, saucers, the sugar bowl and napkins, and arranged an assortment of sweet cakes made by the cook from a recipe that came from Emily's beloved Aunt Lavinia. Then she joined the men in the parlor. Hawthorne was studying a shelf of books while addressing her brother.

"So my name is known to you."

Austin nodded toward Melville. "Both your names."

Melville threw up his hands. "Readers! May Neptune bless you both."

The innocence in the remark led Emily to take stock of Melville. Though the older author was decidedly more distinguished in appearance and manner, and more classically handsome, there was a certain energy—and perhaps even a hint of impropriety—about the younger writer, twelve years older than she, that unsettled her. "I think I may speak for my brother," she said, "in saying we are astonished at having you both here in our parlor."

"And honored," added Austin.

"Nonsense," Melville replied, pleased and embarrassed and looking out the window in the manner of a man disinclined to suffer closed spaces. "We're but scribblers, like the roaming troubadours of old, barely staying afloat. The honor is ours."

"Though not the astonishment," Emily said with a smile.

Melville smiled back looking at her directly for the first time. "That remains to be seen."

"My friend Mr. Melville exaggerates. Much more of a romantic than I, he chafes with more energy against the satisfactions of our actual state," said Hawthorne checking the buttons of his waistcoat.

"What state is that?" Austin asked.

"We are husbands and fathers with small properties and smaller children. Our wilder days are most decidedly in the past."

"Is not there something wild about domesticity, lurking underneath?" asked Emily.

"Not if I can help it, Lord no," Hawthorne replied. "In order for me to go about my work what I most require is peace and tranquility."

"And you Mr. Melville?"

"If I were to answer with honesty, I would say there is wild within all of us, lurking underneath as you say. It is perhaps our most irksome, mysterious and profound characteristic."

"You've a fine and proper library here. But I see no examples of either my nor Mr. Melville's works," said Hawthorne, peeved by Melville's assertion. He succeeded in drawing Emily's attention back to him.

"Our father is a pious gentleman worried about the fate of our souls. You'll find nothing bolder on public view than Professor Hitchcock's Elementary Geology."

"We keep the stronger spirits locked under key," said Austin, "above, within another, less-accessible chamber."

"I consider myself a good Christian," Hawthorne went on. "What literary improprieties of mine merit such banishment?"

"The passions and then the hanging of poor Hepzibah Pyncheon is a stronger draft than this parlor can sanction," Emily answered, pleased with herself.

Hawthorne furrowed his brow somewhat theatrically. "Is this a home then or a church?"

"A bit of both at times," said Austin, "though not today thanks to the absence of the Abbot and Prioress."

"Your most recent work, in my humble opinion, is your best. *The Scarlet Letter* is a masterpiece," Emily said, feeling foolish as she heard it leave her lips.

"I do thank you for that, but all this time I thought we were in Amherst, not Salem."

"In Amherst there are more ministers of the c[
square yard than in any other township."

"Melville here is finishing a work of biblical proportions
that smells of hellfire itself."

"Pray tell," said Austin.

"I do not agree with my mentor's critique."

"Is he your mentor?" Emily asked.

"He has been a most helpful reader and influence."

"I at least believe in Redemption," said Hawthorne.
"Herman doubts the very fabric of the firmament."

"What sort of name is Herman?" Emily asked him with
a smile.

"A very silly one I'm afraid. It's an old German or Nor-
man name meaning 'soldier' or some such thing. In French
I'm told it's Armand."

"Armand Melville. Much better," said Hawthorne.

"Does he always tease you like this?" Emily asked, while
glancing at Hawthorne.

"He's just irked that I have almost finished my book while
he is still in the middle of his next."

"Now that is true," Hawthorne said, liking the way this
sounded.

"And what is your book about Mr. Melville?" asked
Austin. "Could you tell us just a little?"

"I would not know where to begin."

Emily noticed the discomfort once again that was not
entirely modesty but something else.

"It's about a whale," Hawthorne said. "A great white
behemoth that could be the devil, or the Great Almighty."

"An allegory," Austin suggested.

"No. Just a sea table," said Melville. "And factual at that." factual at that."

"Sea tale he says. They'll be using it as kindling in Salem to burn its unfortunate readers," said Hawthorne patting his friend on the back a bit harder than was called for.

It was after tea and out on the porch when Emily mentioned that she had only been to Boston once and never to New York's city. Melville, entranced by the young girl's wit, and Hawthorne, flattered by her reverence, immediately invited brother and sister to accompany them on their journey. Thus began an animated conversation of parries and thrusts, feints and retreats, protests and reconsiderations. In the end, it was an ulterior motive of her brother's that led him to convince her to say yes. Unbeknownst to Emily, Austin's official girl, Susan Gilbert, had a rival, a fellow teacher called Fiona Flanagan who was summering with her modest relations in the town of Fall River. He invented an excuse that would induce their party to reach New York by way of Boston, rather than heading back west. From there, the most agreeable way of making the journey would be via train from Boston to Fall River, where the Bay State Steamboat line had its main port of call. The two writers were amenable to this plan, as they too had friends and family in Boston.

For her part, Emily chose to overcome her somewhat exaggerated preference for remaining in Amherst after quickly surmising that only good could come from her association with two such published men. It was her most fond wish to someday enter their world, if only in a most tangential manner. She also supposed a visit to New York was bound to happen anyway and why not get it over with now in the company of the man she felt closest to, her brother, and these other two gentlemen chaperones who embodied

such depth and experience. The only other time she had
been to Boston was as a girl in her teens, sent there to stay
with friends to recuperate from a nervous relapse, and thus,
she looked forward to replacing that memory with another.

Melville and Hawthorne bid them adieu and went on
their way to stay at an inn the siblings recommended and
where they could leave their horses for the duration. Austin
and his sister set about composing and dispatching letters to
both their parents presenting the most unassailable justifica-
tions they could think of. They all agreed to meet for an
early breakfast at the Dickinson house.

At the inn that evening, over a meal of ham and ale,
Hawthorne and Melville entertained second thoughts.

"I'm not entirely sure what it is we have gotten ourselves
into," Hawthorne said, lighting a pipe. "The household's head
might not take kindly to our magnanimous offer."

"They are both of age and certainly know their parents
better than we," Melville said chewing on a stubborn piece
of gristle.

"I'm certainly in no rush to pass this development on
to Sophia, even though my intentions could not be more
benign nor gentlemanly."

"My lips are sealed."

"And you?"

"I'm in agrement."

"Well, then there you have it! What are we getting ourselves into, man, that we cannot share it with our beloved
spouses?"

Melville only smiled and patted his friend on the shoulder.

In bed that night, while waiting for sleep, Emily felt an
unsettling agitation within, conflicting currents of excitement and regret moving upon a sea of nostalgia for the home

she would be leaving tomorrow. This happened to her each time she went away, even to places as close as Mt. Holyoke in South Hadley where she had gone to school. She did not understand it very well, nor had she much desire to investigate, for the truth was that part of it was pleasurable. The dread was real, but so was the acute awareness of time and place that threatened to break her heart with emotions tangled about where she was and what she possessed. The bed she slept in, the embroidered edges of the pillowcases, her nightgown mother had bought, the solid wooden floor, the oval rug, her writing desk, her things in the closet, all of it there with her now neat and orderly and where they should be. The view out the window of the swaying trees and the cricket sounds. There was a violence to leaving that never ceased to impress her. She was already agonizing over the moment tomorrow morning when she would close the door to this room behind her, knowing how she would try to trick herself into not studying it too carefully before doing so and knowing herself incapable of doing otherwise—that she would look at each and every thing as if it might be for the last time. This reflection led to another she obsessively savored as well. That her room and all of her things placed within it, the house itself and all of its furnishings, the dust resting upon the attic floor, the wax topped jars of blueberry preserves stacked upon the pantry shelf, would remain while she was away, absolutely still, there, whether looked upon by her eyes or not, just in the same way they do when someone dies. And just as sleep began to overtake her, wading through the hazy stream separating consciousness from its darker twin, she remembered all the efforts her grandfather had expended for Amherst and his family, and thanks to which she lay there so safe and surrounded by all that vibrated in consonance with her surname, and then how he had died so far away from home. It sent a shiver through her heart.

5

DURING THE JOURNEY BY STAGE AND TRAIN TO BOSTON the men did most of the talking. Emily was seated next to her brother and the two authors sat opposite. She passed the time listening to them and looking at the scenery. She was impressed by Austin's ability to hold his own with such distinguished minds and she marveled at his confidence in expressing opinions one or the other of his listeners were not always in agreement with. In passing, she also learned that he was far better read than she had assumed.

After stopping for a meal and a chance to refresh themselves, Melville spoke less and less, ceding the floor to Hawthorne and Austin Dickinson who continued their conversation with renewed vigor. Melville alternated between napping and observing Emily. She was tired as well, for she had slept little the night before and she would have gladly shut her eyes too. But the fear of falling asleep and appearing unbecoming kept her sitting ram-rod straight and she was determined to remain that way until they reached their destination. She did not permit her eyes to meet with Melville's although she was keenly aware of his gaze. She did not know what to make of it. She did not feel there was anything vulgar in it. She had had limited experience with that sort of thing and the discomfort she felt at present was different from that provoked by caddish ogling. But neither was the gaze akin to furtive glances she had been subjected to now and again by some of her more hopelessly shy and tongue-tied suitors at Mt. Holyoke and in Amherst.

What was most salient for her was not so much his age, but rather the fact that he was married and that he was the father of almost two children. He was also a man who had consorted no doubt with various brown-skinned maidens on the other side of the world, women who had never touched a book in their life and he had then written about it under a thin guise of fiction in works far more scandalous than anything she had as yet been able to smuggle into her room at home. Whenever Melville's name came up in literary conversation he was deemed a figure doomed by his excess of exoticism. Yet in person he seemed familiar to her. And then, as she set her dark eyes upon a splendid looking farm with not one but two bright red barns, lost in thought about the sort of gentleman he might really be, he in turn took advantage of a particularly agitated exchange between Hawthorne and Austin to break his silence and in subdued tones, to address her.

"Is it normal in Amherst for young men and women to be as well read as you and your brother?"

So accustomed had she grown to being left to her own reveries, the question came as a shock. She froze. It was not so much the question itself that startled her, but rather the fact that he was addressing her at all.

"I'd like to think, Mr. Melville, that in Amherst, all manner of people are well bred."

"'Well read,' I said, not 'well bred'. What do you take me for Miss Dickinson?" he asked her with a smile.

In that second of time, without warning, she could not recall having thought a man as handsome as he looked to her then, leaning slightly forward, amused and grinning, even as she blushed and attempted to banish her embarrassment.

When they arrived in Boston, Hawthorne and Melville went off on their own leaving Austin and Emily to visit with relatives and friends of their family. Austin suggested they spend the night at a hotel but Emily insisted on his taking her to see the flat where he lived, and by the time he overcame his reticence and guided her there it was too late to sleep anywhere else. She was not disappointed. It was a luxury unto itself to get out of her clothes, bathe with a hot damp cloth, put on her night dress, and crawl under one of her brother's moth-eaten blankets taken from his room at home.

Austin, who had spent no small portion of the long day talking, was at it still, as if gripped by a fever. Though somewhat concerned about his state, the sound of his voice also consoled her and enabled her to lie there relaxed and snug as he enumerated his complaints to her about teaching young Irish ruffians. And then, just as sleep was overtaking her, she was stirred awake again by the following. . .

"I have a terrible confession to make, one I ought not to burden you with, but then again you are the only other person in the world I can trust and the torment seething within me is pushing me toward a precipice."

"Oh, Austin."

"You know I have strong feelings for Susan Gilbert."

"I do."

"And that it seems we are all but engaged to be married."

"It has seemed that way to all of us."

"And yet I find my affections distracted by someone else."

"Ah."

"That shocks you?"

"Do I appear shocked?"

"Well, I, for one, am shocked."

"At least half of my life thus far has been consumed by literature, which is a reflection of life, and a significant bulk of its content might be summed up in just such a way."

"So, there you have it."

"I have the essential perhaps, but it is very little. Are you in love with one or the other?"

"I should be in love with Susan."

"Why?"

"Because we are practically engaged. Because we suit each other. Because our families know each other and approve of it all. Because we come from a similar milieu."

"Those may be excellent reasons to hope for a successful marriage, but it does not answer my question."

"I don't know. I go back and forth, like an idiot."

"Does Susan know or suspect anything?"

"No. And it must remain that way."

"Unless and until. . ."

"It's all more complicated than that. This other young woman . . ."

"Do I know her?"

"No. Her name is Fiona."

"She lives here? In Boston?"

"She works here. With me. Teaches at the same school. She's Irish you see and from a humble background."

"Not the sort of match the almighty Dickinsons would favor?"

"Not at all."

"She must have great qualities to recommend her to do battle with all of that."

"She does. Can I be frank with you?"

"You appear to be the very portrait of frankness this evening."

"I mean franker still."

She grabbed the pillow and curled her head around it silently rejoicing in the company of her brother. There was a time that did not seem so long ago when she had observed him bestirred in just the same manner over a kitten that had escaped from his room. He had cried then and implored her to help him. Now he was imploring her again, to listen to his girl trouble.

"Susan's romantic notions, Susan's passion, is all in her head and sweetly expressed in letters and such. Her ideas of love seem to be just that, ideas. There is nothing unusual in this within the society you and I have been born into. It's all very proper and decorous and as it should be. But we are animals you know."

"I know."

"God made us so."

"He did."

"That does not shock you either?"

"I had the very same thought myself the other day."

"It does me good to be able to speak with you about this Emily."

"And me."

"Fiona, who was born into a different sort of society, one in many ways even more morally restricted than ours, is nevertheless a different sort of person. She is, shall we say, more at home with her physicality. And as a result she has awakened my own, in a manner most potent."

Animals indeed, she thought. Contrary to every ballad and poem about love she knew, no one ever mentioned love's reliance upon happenstance, its thoughtless collusion with proximity and chance. When looked at dispassionately it was hard to believe that the person who all of a sudden was transformed from a perfect stranger into the "one and only." The "angel that the gods in their wisdom have caused destiny to bring to me" was invariably the girl next door, an acquaintance's friend, some geographically positioned creature upon whom—when the chemicals did their dance—the same dance surely one observed in those cats that sometimes howl through the night—became miraculously and uniquely suited.

"You fancy her more than you do Susan."

"One opens my mind to the merits of self-criticism, the other boils my blood."

"I see."

"But do you?"

"I think so."

"What am I to do?"

"What boils cools."

"Meaning what exactly."

"I know Susan Gilbert, Fiona no."

"You are talking about reason. I am talking about something else."

"You want to possess this other girl, disrobe her, sate yourself with her. Am I getting closer?"

"Yes."

"Have you ever kissed Susan, I mean truly kissed her?"

"Not yet, no."

"Why not?"

"She never made such an inclination clear to me, and I have never felt bold or compelled enough to go at it on my own initiative. We just write each other about it as something sitting out there like some sugary vision of heaven."

"But you've kissed Fiona."

"Yes."

"And more."

"Yes."

"Assuming she is not a woman of the night . . ."

"Not at all."

"Then what made it so much easier with her?"

"This is what I have been trying to tell you. It just happened. There we were talking about one thing while our eyes were clearly bent upon a different purpose—and then we just reached out to each other as if it were the most natural thing in the world. Which I expect it is."

"You dazzle me brother. Of the urges you speak I know very little. I only appreciate their strength by inference. It seems society, ours at least, is hell-bent against them, lives in constant fear of them, organizes and lays out its norms for the express purpose of containing them. And yet here we are, we and all of God's creatures, because of them. So I fear I am a poor judge of what ails you. I don't pretend to understand it. I only know that our physical demise is just as real as the urges that brought it forth and that it comes upon us with scant regard for our worldly plans. And so to insist on living one's life exclusively in line with what our worldly plans demand is often a folly."

"We might be gone tomorrow."

"Yes. I think of it often."

"Do you really believe in an afterlife, Emily, in a heavenly judgment of our deeds here on earth? I've often observed you in rapture during sermons."

"I like the words and how some men of the cloth string them together. An afterlife—I do not know. In truth, it is hard to imagine despite how blasphemous that must sound."

Herman and Nathaniel paid evening calls accompanying each other to their respective in-laws, the Shaws and the Peabodys. In each of the two households it proved difficult to keep the visit short without offending, and by the time they returned to their hotel, plied with meats, cakes, sweets, and aperitifs neither had any appetite for even the lightest of suppers. Hawthorne retired to his room to write Sophia an account of the day's events. Melville, a man accustomed to walking five or six miles a day, went back out into the Boston summer night and strolled down to the docks.

There were taverns by the wharves and wooden piers, still open and filled with seamen. Two or three of the newer large steamers held the favored moorings, but he went further along to take a gander at the large sailing ships and at a pair of whalers put in for repairs. The smell impregnating the night air, a mixture of dead fish and oily salt water, of tar pitch and ocean brine, brought tears to his eyes. He knew very well that his insomnia was due to the young Dickinson girl. Part of him scoffed at the notion and he assured himself that in the glare of daylight reason would prevail. But he was living the night just then and another corresponding part of him sought temptation and upheaval.

It was here, only some years ago, that he had waited aboard ship, for over a month, had waited to be released from duty after sailing back from the Pacific. And when the day finally came and he stood once again upon America's firmament he had gone directly to call upon the Shaws. He would like to feel that way again about his Lizzie. But time had passed—strange ungraspable time—and now it was someone else he wished to kiss, without knowing why exactly, for the girl was not especially pretty or accomplished at anything he could perceive. And yet he wanted her. All of the symptoms were there. He could not recall having met anyone even vaguely like her.

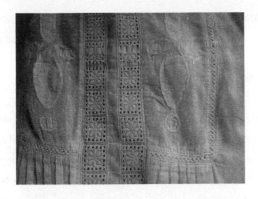

6

ENTERING THE LOBBY ON THE WAY TO THE DINING ROOM for breakfast, Hawthorne and Melville found Emily sitting in a plush chair placed between a potted palm and her black valise. They approached her with furrowed brows.

"Miss Dickinson, what a pleasant surprise," said Hawthorne, taking her hand to almost but not quite kiss it.

"Are we late?" asked Melville, offering her a curt bow.

"Not at all. I am unspeakably early. My brother wished to make a social call in Fall River and took the earliest train. He dropped me here at dawn and has promised to meet us at the pier by two."

"Please join us for breakfast."

"I don't mean to intrude. I'm quite all right sitting here."

"I assure you sitting with us in the dining room will be more congenial."

At breakfast, Hawthorne, largely free of the conflicting emotions besetting his friend, was able to speak impressively and with great wit about the evening before's visits made to the Shaws and Peabodys. As she listened, she entertained another reflection, that earlier that morning she had been seated upon a chamber pot in a small room for that purpose at the end of the hallway adjacent to Austin's flat. Then she had been seated next to her brother on a tram. Then she had sat for two hours in the hotel lobby and now here she was seated once again in this nondescript hotel dining room. She wondered what the point of it was, the moving from one place to the next? To what end? But she was aware as well of the obsessive manner in which these thoughts marched through her head, how difficult it was to stop them and how unsettled they made her feel about further travel. But the die she knew was cast and she would have to go along with them to Fall River at the very least.

Melville—who she observed with some fascination ate an enormous quantity of food—finally interjected some words into the discussion after wiping his lips and beard with a large napkin. "What sort of business would someone like your brother have in a place like Fall River?"

While she did her best to answer Melville's unknowingly awkward question, explaining her brother's motives for seeing Fiona Flanagan that morning, in strictly professional terms, the brother in question lay upon a bare mattress within an abandoned beach cottage off Club Street facing Mt. Hope Bay, watching Fiona undress for him.

Apart from her father who worked at the Metacomet Mill, Fiona Flanagan was the only other earner of wages in her diminished family. Her older brothers Sean and Robert Emmet had both died fighting the Great Fire of 1843. Her

48

beauty was much commented upon in Fall River and her parents wished that as an attractive school teacher she might one day make a good marriage. This was how she justified her relationship with Austin. Having turned down many a suitor from the local mills (and a newspaper vendor she passed each morning on Park Street near Boston's Common), and having permitted only a distant cousin visiting from Cork to kiss her once upon the lips, she had given herself completely to Austin Dickinson. He was handsome, intelligent, a teacher like herself, and the only son of the well-known and prosperous Edward Dickinson of Amherst. The only obstacle she saw in her path, for she was blind to the issue of class distinction, was Austin's official relationship with Susan Gilbert, a woman for whom, it was clear to her, he felt no fire in his belly. His initial reticence had made her bold, and through her attempts to win him over she had discovered how compelling the pleasures of the flesh could be with the appropriate person.

Like an infant who does not tire of watching a face appear and then disappear, each time Fiona shed her clothing, letting dresses and petticoats fall that in spite of their charms had little to do with what they obscured, Austin was shocked and entranced anew upon seeing the reality of her shapely flesh. The tone and tenor of it, the red marks left by the corset stays, the sudden swelling of her breasts, the way her upper thighs, turned away from him as she was just then, blossomed into her thrilling *derriere*, the cracks and crevices, the mysterious animal hairs, the tenderness and bestiality of it causing his heart to race like a frightened deer. As she turned to face him, her face ablush with a sense of shame, her actions clearly contradicted, he thanked Nature itself for having granted him this shard of the present, this pulsating blood. She knelt down beside him, geisha style, her private offering disappearing between her legs, her breasts looming over him, one of her hands placing unruly strands of her long auburn hair behind an ear as the other began to unbutton his briefs, releasing his cock to the humid air. As she took him in her mouth he touched the clean skin of her back with both his hands and watched a reflection of shimmering water against a white wall facing the window stained with mildew.

Two hours later Austin hurried under a hot sun to the Fall River Line pier where *The Empire State* was docked, boilers lit and taking on passengers. The tryst had ended on an awkward and troublesome note. Enthralled the two of them during his final thrusting, he slipped out of her bottom and found himself in a more customary, less controversial, but— biologically speaking—far more volatile corridor just as he began to ejaculate. Fiona arched her back in pain, suddenly a virgin no more, as he did his best to withdraw. But the damage was done and a large army of Dickinson spermatozoa had been launched, furiously struggling upstream to spawn. The couple clung to each other before dressing—swearing eternal love, putting a brave face on what might well end up becoming a disaster for the both of them. As he strolled along the shore road, now more relieved than anything else to be away from a place where he had been so happy just hours earlier, he weighed the odds for fertilization based on no practical knowledge of the matter.

As his anxiety increased, the figure of Susan Gilbert, so disparaged while he and Fiona sated themselves, so impossible to imagine naked and moaning—as impossible to imagine as his own parents engaged in the same activity, which good grief, they actually *had* done, for there he was, he and his two sisters—came back to him like a balm, a sanctuary to seek refuge within, a proper dress clean and pressed to hold on to. Suddenly, he wanted only to renew his courtship with added respect, to attend services with her at the Arch Street Presbyterian Church, seeking celestial forgiveness for his wantonness. He wished to be his father's son, and so what in God's name was he doing accompanying Emily on a trip to New York their father would surely disapprove of? All of it had been due to his scheming weakness. Not even Emily really wanted to go—he knew her well enough to see that— she was just trying to be a sport so that he would think well of her. The knavery of it all!

And so it went—his heart pounding from fear of being found out if poor Fiona should be with child. But as the ship came into view and slowing his pace, realizing he was on time, another side of him fought to make a case for reason and for his own nature. From where was such subservient cowardice emanating? What had he done that was wrong? Which God was actually paying attention to his womanizing and why? What would a life be like, year after year, with Susan Gilbert in his bed and his father and mother living across the street? Was the coziness of Thanksgiving dinner or a familial reunion on Christmas Eve worth all of the proper drudgery required?

All four members of the traveling party boarded the Empire State with some misgivings that day. It was only once the ship set forth with many of its passengers waving good-bye to those left behind, parasols mixing with straw boaters, the water of the bay clean and clear, the sea grass and low dunes along the less inhabited sections of shore shimmering under the benevolent July sun, that the futility and sterility of their own too-worried minds gave way to the physical beauty of the external world and to a realization of their present good fortune to be in it.

After settling their belongings in their respective state-rooms and meeting again astern to take tea as the ship made its way down to Newport, they were beginning to relax and enjoy themselves—Emily especially in light of the novelty this outing defined. At precisely this juncture, they were set upon by an unsolicited bore wearing a clerical collar, carrying, in a manner for all to notice, a sorry looking Holy Bible. Unbidden, he addressed them.

"What a fine and fitting new land of milk and honey these New England shores and coves are to behold. The Lord God of Abraham blesses us with such abundant riches."

All four captive listeners remained mute, entertaining the collective hope that the exclamation might be a non sequitor. But the exclaimer took their silence, as bores are apt to do, as acquiescence and even encouragement for his peculiar train of thought. Emily knew, merely by the look of his sensible and too-worn shoes, the sort of man before them—dull, intrusive, clumsy, immensely certain and self-satisfied armed with a bushel basket of homilies repeated ad nauseam without a tinge of shame. On he went.

"As compensation for this bountiful gift it befalls upon we of the True Faith to enlighten the natives and lesser races who continue to prance about like vermin on these verdant virgin lands."

Her parents would have stood for it, out of decorum, bearing up in a courteous fashion, and she of course with them. Given his druthers she imagined Hawthorne would have simply bowed and exited the scene. Her brother Austin, whose matinal activities she refused to imagine even though she could hardly think of another thing, would have taken the man on his own terms, looking to reason and to complementary and more convincing scriptures with which to parry the other's too headed certainty. In fact, she could see Austin wetting his lips as he often did before speaking, preparing to do just that. But it was Melville who interceded first and, in a manner for her, entirely unexpected.

"What the deuces are you talking about man? Get on with you. Who in their right mind should have to stand for such drivel on a day as fair as this?"

"I am the right reverend Josiah Huffington and who are you sir to behave in such a rude and bullish way?"

Melville strode right up to the man.

"I am the anti-Christ with native American blood in my veins disposed to toss you over the side this very second if you do not remove yourself to another part of this ship straight away."

"Well, I never . . ."

But retreat he did in a Huffington huff, clutching the Bible with renewed fervor, backing off and then turning away from Melville's intimidating demeanor. Hawthorne, upstaged yet again by his companion but not yet sure how their audience of two might react, patted his friend on the shoulder. "Herman, you are a genius." Melville smiled, turned, and looked at Austin and Emily. "I'm not as mean as that. I just knew it was either that or be saddled with him for an hour."

Austin, frustrated by not being able to lock horns with the man shot a question to the author instead.

"Do you really have Indian blood in you, Mr. Melville?"

"Not a drop, unfortunately."

"Unfortunately?"

"My family, as do all of yours, goes back. My father never tired of reminding me of our royal ancestors in Scotland but we have been here since the first waves of colonists landed and we all call ourselves Americans and gaze with unwarranted condescension upon any newcomers. But we are all newcomers. The original Americans are its Indians and they are still its most authentic custodians."

"But they are not Christians," said Emily with a malicious smile.

"Anti-Christ. That was a good one," said Hawthorne.

"My own theory about what it means, or should mean to be a Christian, is a simple one: 'Blessed are the pure of heart, for they will see God.'"

"But what might it mean to be pure of heart?" she asked.

The stern's upper deck where they were gathered was made from finely varnished wooden boards and a white canvas awning stretched over them keeping the airy salon in shade. A gull flew along with them, hovering for a spell before veering off, shoreward, then coming to a fluttery rest upon a gentle swell.

"I'd like to think any Wampanoag native waking in the shelter of a wild blueberry shrub is pure of heart—or was . . ." He paused and looked at Emily directly. "I'd go as far as to say that you, Miss Dickinson, are pure of heart. Have you seen God?"

Hawthorne jumped in. "You see, he *is* the anti-Christ after all—pronouncing one blasphemy after the other."

Melville smiled but ignored the comment and repeated his question. "Have you seen God Emily?"

It was the first time he had called her that and it cut her to the quick—catching her once again unprepared. It was as if the organ that was her heart, pure or otherwise and apart from its own rhythmic beating, skipped of its own accord to the side. To mask the feeling she turned from him and from the rest of them, placing her hands upon the railing and looked down at the water of Mt. Hope Bay, Then she looked over her shoulder and answered him.

"I wonder if perhaps I might be seeing Him right now."

Her brother made the connection immediately.

"My sister has never seen salt water before. She has never been on a boat or ship."

She turned around.

"I'm just a local girl, gentlemen, an Amherst maiden unaccustomed to any body of water larger than Lake Warner in North Hadley. I am overwhelmed."

"Then what you are seeing now is but the Archangel Gabriel," said Melville.' "God you will see later, just before the evening meal once we've left Newport and are out on the open sea a bit before setting a course through the more sheltered sound of Long Island."

"There you go, blaspheming again," said Hawthorne. "I, too, have the greatest respect for the oceans Melville but to call it 'God' . . ."

"I think he means—it is certainly what I meant," said Emily in a meek tone, "is that the wonder of the seas reflects the majesty of God."

"Well put sister."

"I can agree with that," said Hawthorne. "But is that what you meant, Herman?"

"My God hath not long flowing hair or any resemblance to mankind at all. That presumptuous fantasy for me is a form of blasphemy."

"Your God is your great white whale—a massive creature filled with vengeance."

"God—whatever that word really means, is to my mind, not only a reflection of nature's wonders but nature herself, all of it, the living and the dead, all that crawls, and swims, and grows from the soil and sand and all that simply exists upon the earth inanimate and immovable."

Austin took flight.

"I believe the term for a man of your beliefs is 'pantheist.' You are an adherent of 'pantheism.' It has a noble tradition, going back to the Greeks."

"I'll settle for that," said Melville. "If only to put an end to anymore discussion about religion."

"Amen," said Emily.

But Austin and Hawthorne had yet to be sated. "I think it a fine and fitting topic," the latter enjoined. "As do I," said the former.

"And why, I pray, might that be?" Melville inquired.

"Religion's hold upon us is such because life ends," Emily said.

The Empire State docked at Newport taking on provisions and additional passengers. Before retiring below in order to avoid all of the on-deck commotion, Melville noticed ships from the diminishing slave trade owned by the family of the late and despicable James de Wolf but kept the observation to himself. He rested in his stateroom reading and then fell asleep, not waking until the ship was underway again. Refreshed and back on deck, he watched the Prudence Island lighthouse being left behind. It was twilight. Salmon and violet tones graced all the eye could see, including Emily and Austin who he spotted in conversation up by the prow.

"Are your feelings any clearer brother?"

"No. When I first saw Fiona this morning, a morning that now feels like it took place a week ago, I could think of no one else. Then, as I took my leave I was beset with grief and remorse and with stark lucidity I saw the error of my ways and only wished to do whatever is required to secure the hand of Susan. And then an hour after that, just before I reached the dock, I found myself yearning once again for Fiona and viewing my sudden reversion to craving an orderly life with Susan as an act of moral cowardice."

"And now?"

"Now I am relieved to be away from the both of them!"

"I wonder why you cannot conceive of 'an orderly life' with Fiona, simply because she is Irish and not a member of our dour Amherst social circuit? I wonder to what extent her very unsuitability provides in your mind the crucial grain of sand, thus creating a pearl of desire for you?"

He looked at his sister, born barely a year after he, in a new light. His innards filled simultaneously with affection for her and humiliation directed toward himself.

"Ahoy there."

They turned and found the figure of Melville, a portrait of calm and confidence. Austin returned the greeting.

"Hello."

"I don't mean to interrupt anything."

"Not at all," said Austin, "You are in truth rescuing me from the tenacious tentacles of my sister's probing mind."

"Tenacious tentacles?" she repeated, feeling the color entering her cheeks and hating it.

"Not an image I would associate with your sister."

"But accurate nevertheless."

"I realized we were heading out into the ocean and in this extraordinary light. Impossible to remain in one's stateroom."

"Well if you will both excuse me," Austin said, "it is to my stateroom I must retire."

"Must you?" Emily asked.

He nodded to them both. "See you at supper then in half an hour."

And then he left them. An awkward silence ensued, until Melville pointed out to sea so that she turned to take in the view.

"Look," he said. "The face of God, or that of Oceanus at the very least."

"Would it not be that of Poseidon, or of his Roman equivalent, Neptune?"

"Poseidon was associated with the Mediterranean only and Neptune, in the end, by many at least, with bodies of fresh water. But when Odysseus and Nestor walk together along the shore of the sea in the Iliad, their prayers are addressed 'to the great sea-god who girdles the world.' It is to Oceanus, not to Poseidon, that their thoughts are directed. But let's just look. In that direction it is all open sea—the deep Atlantic."

With the waning light a breeze was blowing, particularly there near the bowsprit, nullifying the noise made by the engines and the massive midship paddles. She gripped the wooden banister of the railing tightly, to stem the sense of vertigo the view brought with it. Never had she felt so adrift, so on a precipice. The sea did not end. There was only the gradually darkening horizon that helped to make it seem so. She understood how men for ages, upon contemplating this same sight, had naturally assumed the Earth to be flat and that sailing too far away from the land's safety, one would eventually fall off into a dark and frightful universe much as Lucifer and his hosts of angels had. Melville covered her hand with one of his own. She looked at it—at their hands together—her right hand under his left. Then he withdrew it but neither of them forgot it.

"It is too much for me," she said. "Too vast, too open."

There were tears in her eyes. He spoke to her very gently.

"We're closer to land than perhaps it seems to you. We are in no danger."

"We're surrounded by water, deep and cold and filled with all of those creatures you write about and have dealt with on your ocean travels—and I cannot swim."

7

Where is the Bee—
Where is the Blush—
Where is the Hay?—

Ah, said July—
Where is the Seed—
Where is the Bud—
Where is the May—
Answer Thee—Me—

EMILY WOULD WRITE THESE LINES YEARS LATER. BUT
tonight her twenty-year-old self awakened of a sudden
before dawn. Upon remembering where she was her heart
accelerated. The entire stateroom, small, dark, and humid,
was vibrating from the force of the steam engines hidden in

the bowels. And it swayed as well, back and forth, up and down—gently but unceasingly. She sat up and looked out her porthole and saw the water only a few feet below. All else was darkness. Overcome with sadness for the room and bed that with each revolution of the paddles lay farther and farther behind, she rose and dressed.

The Empire State, 440 feet long and 90 feet wide, moved upon the waters. The shorelines to either side, made from cobble beaches, coastal bluffs of glacial deposits, rocky head-lands, and tidal wetlands, loomed invisible in the dark. Fresh waters fed into the sound from the Connecticut River, the Housatonic, the Thames, and the Nissequogue. Pines and scrub oak, beach plum and rose hip bushes began where the beaches ended. Under the vessel's barnacle-studded gliding hull lived oysters and lobsters, bluefish and striped bass, win-ter flounder and fluke . . . scup . . . tautog . . . weakfish.

A few gas lamps in the lounges were still lit lending an eerie glow to the velvet banquettes. She found a steward asleep slouched upon an easy chair. Desperate for fresh air she chose the first exit and, climbing two flights of stairs, made her way up to the weather deck. It was there she saw a man alone leaning into the breeze. He sensed her presence, turned, and smiled.

"Emily."

"Mr. Melville."

"What are you doing up at this hour?"

"My room is so warm—oppressive. And what about you?"

"I am often awake at this hour—to feed my cows."

She joined him and the air was cool and the light the way it is just before actual light appears. And as she came up near to him he took her by both shoulders, leaned forward, and kissed her on the lips. For the first few seconds she just stood there, unclear about how to react. And then he took her in his arms, moved his head back and looked into her eyes and then he kissed her again. This time she kissed him back. It was when she did this that he experienced a surge of happiness he would long remember. He looked at her again. She looked back at him. Keeping an arm around her they both faced the sea and watched as the first hints of dawn emerged from the east.

Hours later a pensive Nathaniel Hawthorne, dressed and his bag strapped shut, rested in his stateroom before breakfast. What had been his initial intention of spending a pair of carefree summer weeks with Melville away from their lovely wives and children before he and Sophia moved away from Lenox seemed to have been thwarted. It was, he realized, partly his own damn fault. What had begun as a social call to Amherst, one he himself had imposed, had turned, initially, into a harmless and amusing escapade. He had envisioned the four of them as characters in a novel of manners, not as men and women made of flesh and blood.

And he genuinely believed that Melville had shared in this same spirit. But clearly something had changed. He would have to speak to Melville about it, a prospect that did not in any way please him. Surely the girl's chatty brother had noticed and surely, in spite of the young man's weakness for he and Melville's literary fame, he was mature enough to warn his sister against giving Melville anything resembling hope for his increasingly obvious love making. He wondered how things might be between Melville and his wife Elizabeth? She was a smart and handsome woman, not a beauty, but neither was the Dickinson girl. At least Elizabeth was a fully formed person quite dedicated it seemed to her husband's pursuits and decidedly patient with the man's grueling writing routines . . . or so it seemed. Who knew what really went on in their bed, in that household with so many other people about? And then there was Melville's nature. What sort of a fellow, born a gentleman into two upstanding families, leaves his native soil, sails away to the farthest regions imaginable, as a common whaler, only to abandon ship to live (and cavort!) on a jungle island among naked savages with no morals or decorum at all? A sort different than he. A sort capable of anything. Granted he himself often felt constrained in a social sense by his Calvinist creed but he would never go as far as to pronounce aloud the kind of heresies Melville had fired off yesterday afternoon.

He supposed the girl found his friend's thirst for danger and his equally dangerous religious views compelling in some fashion—the way perfectly well-bred women sometimes profess a weakness for ruffians or condemned criminals. But finding such murky behavior attractive and getting enmeshed in it were two different things. Yes, he would have to arrange a talk with Melville about it that very day.

The breakfast service finished as the ship passed between Sand's Point and Great Neck. Melville was nowhere to be seen and Hawthorne, relieved, finished his eggs and trout sitting with the Dickinsons. Emily ate only a sweet roll with a cup of tea and she marveled at the variety and amounts of food the surrounding passengers were stuffing into their mouths. Her brother and Mr. Hawthorne seemed to be similarly ravenous. But just as she prepared in her mind to censure the whole hoggish lot she remembered how Melville too had consumed vast quantities of food the morning before and it caused her to smile.

He had kissed her. They had kissed. She had been kissed alone at sea by an attractive married man, an author and adventurer—the whole thing ludicrously inappropriate— and thrilling. Of course he had not come to breakfast. She had been dreading seeing him as well. For, now what? Now that the sun was up and the day begun and everyone dressed and talkative about their business once again. She had often noticed how differently one felt things during the night.

They found Melville, unusually withdrawn, standing by his bag midship as the marshes and farmland of Lesser Minneford Island came into view. He nodded to Hawthorne, shook Austin's hand, and limited his final salutation to a simple "Miss Dickinson." As time went by she ceased finding his silences annoying until she began to realize she found them compelling. It was an intimate silence that said many things.

Then they were off the coast of White Stone, the fat western end of Long Island, navigating south toward Randal's Island, the last bastion of wilderness before Manhattan came into view. And soon the waterway narrowed as they entered into the East River proper. Off the port side of the steamer was Blackwell Island—a thin arrangement of vegetable gardens raked and hoed at either end of the penitentiary and the insane asylum looming there. When Hawthorne identified these two buildings to Emily she found herself unable to look anywhere else. As Hawthorne droned on, gesturing starboard, showing off his knowledge of Manhattan's wilder rural tracts, peppering in anecdotes and literary asides, Austin taking it in like a child, Melville still sullen and statuesque, she studied the off-putting brick constructions and their barred windows. It was difficult to distinguish the prison from the asylum until a young woman appeared at one of the upper windows facing the water, close enough to the ship so that Emily could make out the girl's dark straggly hair. She cried out to the passersby at full volume, "Shit, shit, shit, shit! We're all made of shit! God is shit! It will soon be raining piss and shit!"

Emily became aware of people snickering around her. One man, well attired, indignant, and to no avail, yelled back at her to be quiet. From the lower decks she heard many of the passengers laughing at the woman, as if this Bruegelian bit of side show fare had been organized for their benefit. Emily said nothing and remained transfixed, keeping her eyes on the woman even as the steamer left her in its wake. Hawthorne was making an iron-willed effort to ignore the whole unseemly spectacle, persisting with his Manhattan travelogue with such energy and increased volume Austin did not dare look away. But Melville did, watching and listening, and he noted Emily's distress and it softened him and drew him out of his state of self-absorption. He touched her forearm, covered with a black cotton coat sleeve, distracting her from her anguish. Without turning to look at him she in turn touched his hand and squeezed it with gratitude before letting go. She spoke to him in a low tone.

"Why are they laughing? It's horrid."

"Fear I expect."

"Fear."

"The sort that elicits cruelty, as a mask."

Then she did turn to him, looking into his eyes once again for the first time since they had held each other that dawn.

"Fear of what?"

"Of how little distance separates their so-called sanity from such a state of raving."

"Do you really think so?"

"I've seen men go mad overnight. Tough common an officer once. Seemingly normal one day, ranting the next without any apparent or obvious affliction or explanation, no fever, no medieval draughts or humors wafting over the ship. Are there no lunatics in Amherst?"

She smiled. "A few. Including a man who had the revolting habit of repeatedly exposing his person in a most vulgar fashion. But his family cares for him."

"A much kinder solution than this one, no? We have a boy not right in the head in our household, a nephew of mine."

"What were they thinking building a mad house next to a prison?"

"I don't know."

Hawthorne finally had to admit he had lost half his imagined audience. He went quiet. The rapidly approaching end to their journey fixed all of their attention upon the shores. Brooklyn and her church spires to the left, Manhattan a mess of masts and commerce to the right. With each block traveled further south the river became increasingly crowded with other ships and crafts of all description; frigates and ferries, sloops and schooners, scows and canoes. The day was warm and the water level low and congested with garbage and injudiciously pumped bilge. For the rest of her life Emily would associate her arrival to New York with the vile screams of the poor mad woman and the putrid fumes ascending from the waters and the piers mixing together in the July heat.

In typical fashion, Melville only began to contemplate where he might stay in the city moments before the steamer docked. His brother Allan had moved his wife and two babies up to a house at 31st Street, on the very frontier with

Canada as far as he was concerned. His own house on Fourth Avenue at Eleventh Street had finally been sold—at a significant loss—a year earlier. What Melville wished for was privacy and he thus determined to find a hotel close to his old neighborhood and near to the Duyckinck brothers and their wives who lived on Clinton Place. Sarah and Rowland Morewood also lived close by. If he were to keep himself from further courting Miss Dickinson he had best be surrounded by his customary coterie of friends and acquaintances.

The Empire State moored at Pier 14 at Fulton Street. Emily saw three dead rats floating in the water as she disembarked. The pier was splintery and the air humid and the dock teemed with passengers and street vendors, teamsters and drays loading and unloading goods. Melville hailed a carriage and then had to argue for it with another customer who tried to get there before him. He held the door open for Austin and Emily. Austin shook his hand.

"You must come with Mr. Hawthorne this afternoon to have tea with our father."

"I shall do all I can to be there," he replied, only glancing briefly at Emily.

The carriage rattled off upon newly laid cobblestones as Hawthorne and Melville walked west, pushing their way past three scavenging sows before reaching a shady and quieter portion of the street.

"As luck would have it," Melville said, "my printer's shop is right on this street at number 112. I might as well go there directly, do my business, and be done with it. If you don't mind accompanying me, we can relax together afterward."

Robert Craighead's shop was found on Fulton between William and Nassau Streets. An oyster cart was parked out front, owned and administered by a redheaded freckle-skinned man wearing a soiled blue apron serving his goods from a barrel filled with ice along with pitchers of warm ale. Melville, his mind encumbered with The Whale and his dilemma, hardly noticed the fellow. But Hawthorne, looking on some level to reduce the importance of his friend's literary project, fixed his gaze on the oyster vendor and had a sudden urge to write about him as Dickens might.

"How is business sir?"

"A bit slow a the moment, your grace, but come an hour from now you'll see a mighty line a-formin'."

"Are you from Ireland?"

"That I am—from County Clare."

"Which is . . ."

"On the west coast, the wild coast, poor and rugged and softly green."

"And did you sell oysters there as well?"

"To tell you the truth, I can't abide them, but here they sell quicker than rosaries in the Vatican. In Ireland, I fished salmon from the Shannon and did just fine till slain by a lass from Dingle."

Though impatient to speak with Craighead, Melville, intrigued by the oysterman's palaver, entered the fray.

"When I was a boy here . . ."

"Were you born here sir?"

"Right on this island, just a few blocks from here."

"Is that a fact? So you are a 'native' New Yorker—the very first one I've met."

"When I was a boy we'd dive for oysters in the Hudson. The water was crystal clear then like it was when the first settlers arrived."

"Is that a fact? Tiz an odd bit of victual indeed. So much labor for so little gain."

"Tell us about the lass from Dingle," Hawthorne said, buying a glass of the ale.

"There I was, slammin a salmon upon a rock, minding my own p's and q's when . . . this was mid-March, mind you . . . when I seen this vision in skirts up to her ankles in cold Shannon brine, leanin over, presenting mine eyes with the finest roundest callin' card a man could wish for. Pickin' daffodils she was to sell at market."

"And where is Dingle?"

"Tiz a testicle hangin', from the great emerald cock of Ireland—to the south of me—a full day's travellin'. So as you might suspect I struck up a conversation with her. Katherine was her name, Katherine Hanratty her name now."

"You being Mr. Hanratty."

"That's a fact. And when I found out where she was from I said to her, 'Well, that would explain it.' 'Explain what?' she says. 'Explains why it is I've never seen ye here before, because if I had, I would surely have made it my business to have known you earlier.' 'Are you talking dirty to me now?' she says. 'I swear I'm not,' says I. Then she says, 'Then what's all this about 'knowin'? I've read the Bible and 'know' a thing or two.' But this she said with a grin on her face, a grin that'd light up the caves of Carthage."

The caves of Carthage, thought Hawthorne—now there's a title. Melville excused himself and went into the shop and found Craighead setting type with two assistants at the very back of the establishment. The three of them wore aprons as well, white once upon a time and now stained with years of ink. Black ink and the smell of metal and oil infused the air.

"Ahoy there, Ahab," said the printer as he always did upon seeing his guest so that Melville could answer, "Call me Ishmael." The men shook hands and the assistants nodded gravely with a look of respect not lost upon the author. Spending most of their time ruining their eyes and fingers setting type for simplistic pamphlets for and against the abolitionists, it was rare for them to be engaged in the creation of actual literature. He smiled at them as Craighead took him by the arm and escorted him up a flight of stairs to his office.

"I was just making some coffee. Would you care for some?"

"I would. I've just stepped off the steamer from Boston in which I was barely able to sleep. I've brought you more copy."

"Excellent news. And I've more proofs for you to take back with you."

"It's almost finished. One more month's labor and I'll have the last of it for you."

It was Craighead's chief assistant, Cyrus Clark, who greeted Hawthorne when he entered the shop some minutes later.

"Can I help you sir?"

"I'm here with Herman Melville."

"Ah. He's upstairs with Mr. Craighead at present."

"Well then I'll join them."

"Might I announce you first sir—or Mr. Craighead will be at me throat after you've all departed."

"Nathaniel Hawthorne."

Clark looked at him more closely.

"You wouldn't be pulling a man's leg by any chance?"

"I've never been a leg-puller, sir."

71

"No, sir. Well, it is in honor indeed to have you here. I won't be but a second."

The midday meal took place with the Duyckinck brothers—George and Everet—the four men waxing expansive about a round table at the Knickerbocker Pub.

"I see I am outnumbered," said Melville toward the meal's end, sipping at a glass of port. "But I do admire your optimism, the way you speak about American literature, the new American literature, as if this were England."

"England's the past, man," said George, his superficial nasal capillaries aglow. "England's a dying, selfish, sclerotic father and we're his vigorous, rebellious sons."

"Here-here!" said Hawthorne, feeling the effects of more alcohol than he was used to imbibing, especially at that hour of the day. He just then realized that Melville, save his thimbleful of fortified wine, had yet to touch a drop that day of anything other than coffee and water. Everet grabbed the baton from his brother.

"James Fenimore Cooper-Herman. Longfellow, Emerson, Nathaniel here, yourself man. All of you fresh and young and new and strong."

"Fresh and new and strong. I'll grant you that. But this is a still young nation, filled with fur trappers and woodsmen, small businessmen, farmers, and tobacco chewers—slave holders! The world you dream aloud about here is unique to this busy little island. I cannot vouch for Nathaniel, but it says all that needs to be said that a writer like myself, who works the pen day in and out, year after year, remains in terrible debt and receives but a pittance for his labors. I think your dying sclerotic sire across the drink has a lot to be said for him still."

Their waiter appeared, presenting the bill. Melville could not have timed the revelation of his monstrous debts any better and he pretended to fish about in his trouser pockets like an expert as the two brothers studied the docu ment and prepared to do their bit for the cause.

"Put your money away, Herman. You too, Nathaniel. This one is on us and with great pleasure."

"Much obliged," said Hawthorne.

"I'll not hear of it," said Melville.

"Oh yes, you will," said Everet, staying Melville's wrist.

"Well, I do thank you then, and I propose you and your lovely wives and children come to the Berkshires and visit with us, and I'll take you on a grand tour of the rural America at who's altar you both worship."

"Capital idea," said Hawthorne.

"Come next month," said Melville, "Before the summer escapes us."

"I'll come too, along with my son Julian. What do you say, gentlemen?"

"Why, yes, of course."

"Absolutely," said George. "Any opportunity to abandon this soiled urban isle to breathe the pastoral Arcadian air you two gentlemen share would be a tremendous thrill."

The four men emerged onto the bright, oppressively warm street. Hawthorne with his country squire look, the brothers suffering in sweat under their black coats. Melville was wearing his customary loose-fitting garb, part shepherd, part Parisian painter.

"Duyckinck," said Hawthorne. "What the deuce sort of Dutch name is that?"

"A most unfortunate one," said Evert. "You can't imagine the range of mispronunciations we have to put up with."

"All of them most understandable," said George, "considering how it looks on paper."

"My favorite is *Dewy-kin-ick*! It might be Gaelic or Welsh, meaning 'Get thee away from me!'"

"Or how about, '*Do-you-think*'? I rather like that one."

"It's primarily 'due' to the sixty guilders paid to the Indians by Peter Minuit back in 1626 that our family ended up here at all. Otherwise we'd still be bankrupt tulip brokers in Leiden."

Melville smiled at their banter without paying it much attention. He was looking up the block from where they stood at a house he had lived in with his parents, brothers, sisters, and servants many years ago. He remembered his father's gaiety and wit and absurd powers of denial in the face of the debts he so cavalierly racked up year after year and tears came into his eyes and a lump formed in his throat, and as he noticed thunder clouds forming, coming down the Hudson from up north, he remembered holding his own son in his arms just the other day by the lake and holding Emily that morning.

Upon their arrival at the front desk of the elegant Everett House dominating the northeastern edge of Union Square Park at Seventeenth Street and Broadway, the Dickinson siblings were handed a sealed letter on house stationery.

My Dearest Austin and Emily,

I must reiterate my displeasure at this most unfortunate adventure you have undertaken without consulting your parents who, believe it or not, still know far more about these things, and about the world in general, than either of you. It is thus doubly unsettling that, owing to my venerable duties as a representative of our Commonwealth, I find

*myself compelled to travel this very morning to Washington.
It causes me great frustration and worry to have missed your
arrival to Manhattan and I shudder at the thought of what
your dear mother will think, of you both, and of me (!) upon
learning of this latest contretemps.*

*Thus it falls upon me to tell you, urge you, to order you
(!) to return to Amherst. Having come this far I will allow
you both to have a look around the City of New York, but you
must stay at this, my hotel, no longer than two nights, in the
adjacent rooms already reserved for you. You are to take all
of your meals here as well. I have already paid for such a plan
and I am leaving you some extra monies to be spent wisely. I
do expect you to take advantage of this opportunity in a dili-
gent and judicious manner—in a manner far more judicious
than the one you have thus far demonstrated.*

*I have written to your mother of all this and she will
expect you back home no later than Friday afternoon. I
entrust the safety and honor of your sister to you Austin—
need I say more?*

Your disappointed, but still affectionate father

"Oh dear," said Emily reading it over her brother's shoulder, "Mr. Hawthorne will be most vexed."

"No more vexed than I," said Austin, stuffing the letter
into his coat pocket without taking the trouble to refold it. "I
refuse to be treated this way, as if I were a boy of ten."

"Don't take it to heart. That is how they still see us, I'm
afraid. And frankly, I'm a bit relieved he is not here."

Leaving her brother to recover from his sulk, Emily
asked for pen and paper and wrote forthwith to both their
parents employing only the most respectful and saccharine

terms. She had never had a hotel room to herself before and found the prospect exciting. Austin washed up and offered to escort her around the neighborhood but Emily set him loose upon his own devices, preferring to recuperate the sleep she had lost the night before, and arranged to meet him in the Everett House lobby in time for tea with their travel companions.

Left alone, she undressed and put on a nightgown and sat by her fourth floor window looking down at the park. There was a fine fountain at its center and there were luxurious private houses constructed at either side and tall leafy trees were in full bloom, covering paths and gardens and banquettes for strollers-by. Carriages clip-clopped to and fro and from the dizzying height of her perch it all appeared to her like some painting in the sort of grand museum she had read about but never visited.

As she continued to look, replaying the events that took place upon the weather deck of the steamer that dawn, free at last from interruption, the leaves of the trees gracing the retinas of her eyes began to rustle. Clouds appeared, large and dark, and in the distance, a rumbling. The downy hairs on her forearms stood up and her nipples tensed as the light upon that urban landscape changed from clear and unrelentingly bright to more somber hues, cooler, charged, and textured. And as the clouds drew closer and bore down bringing moist breezes and dropping temperatures, the leaves began to turn over, ceding their green backs to the fluttering silvery undersides just before it began to pour. As some of the rain splattered against the windowpane, ricocheting against her face and neck and dampening the thin cotton of her gown, she realized she was happy. It caught her by surprise.

She consecrated the moment—and held on to it. How could a kiss do such a thing? What manner of creature were we?

She sat there transfixed and wondered whether it might be a further reflection upon what she feared to be a declining sense of her morality, that she was entertaining the thought, all of a sudden, as the rain came down, that her father's exquisitely timed and continuing absence might have another explanation. "Venerable duties" had been the official excuse proffered. But "venerable" she knew came from "venerate," which came from the Latin "venerari" that, in turn, had its root in the goddess Venus, from "vener" . . . to love . . . to desire. What traces of flesh and blood dwelled beneath the well-pressed clothing her father wore? It was not the first time she had pondered his sensuality, kept so restrained. Would her mother still be receptive to him? Such a thing was hard indeed to imagine. Lavinia had been born eighteen years ago. Their house was too crowded, every and all noises painfully evident through the papered planked pine. But her father *was* a man, a man like his own sinning son, a man like the married authors, both of them fathers too, and one of whom had actively flirted with her and the other had kissed her!

Could it be true? Who might such a woman be, to pull her father away from Amherst? Was it another man's daughter? . . . obviously . . . or maybe a woman of dubious character . . . an actress . . . a dancer!

Hawthorne and Melville waited out the worst of the downpour at the Duyckinck residence on Clinton Place before taking their leave, promising to attend a supper party that evening at the mansion of Rowland and Sarah Morewood. The rain had dwindled to an intermittent drizzle as the two men took a small detour on their way to Union Square and the Everett House. What had been ten acres of farmland with a stream running through it when the Dutch first colonized Manhattan was now a public park. Once it had been sublet to freed slaves in exchange for their agreeing to keep Native Americans at bay. Then it became a potter's field and place of execution. Its penultimate use had been to serve as the Washington Military Parade Ground where local militias trained and exhibited their finery. This most recent renovation was just two years old. Fine homes had been built about the perimeter and neither Melville nor Hawthorne had seen it yet. It was here, wandering through its walks and gardens, a more intimate version of what had been done at Union Square, that Hawthorne got up the necessary nerve to broach the topic that had been nagging at him since early morning.

"Do you remember our conversation the other evening at the Inn at Amherst?"

"Why?"

"Well it seemed to me then we were both a bit stirred, surprised, and a bit wary as well by the invitation we had just made to the young Dickinsons."

"I remember."

"What I most vividly recall was an owning up to the realization that we were, neither of us, eager to let our spouses in on it."

"On what?"

"On the fact that we had just asked a young, unmarried girl to accompany us on our journey."

"A young girl accompanied as well by her own brother, on a trip that had as one of its purposes a meeting with their esteemed father, a meeting we are about to consummate."

"Consummate you say?"

"I fail to see what you are driving at, Nathaniel. And fur thermore, what I also remember was the spirit in which you wrote that second note to me, bidding us both to enjoy an adventure together before you and Sophia move away. Well, here we are, in the thick of it, not an adventure exactly, at least by my definition, but thus far a thoroughly enjoyable sojourn, no?"

"All true. You do have a very good point there. What I am driving at, however, and I hope you will pardon me if I seem tactless, is the state of your affections for Emily."

This induced Melville to stop, at the juncture just where Fifth Avenue began.

"The state of my affections?"

"I am no fool, man, especially when it comes to human behavior. Back at that inn we were innocents, men pretending to be rouges, playing at it if only for the simple pleasure it afforded us that went well with the idea of our mutual 'escape' from married life."

"Do get to the point, man."

"Do you fancy her?"

"We both fancied her."

"We both fancied her, or so I thought, the way men, or women for that matter, fancy a comely stranger passing by, but certainly no more than that."

"I find her absolutely charming."

"But what are your intentions?"

"One would think you were a close relation, Nathaniel. Are you a cousin, or the girl's uncle by any chance?"

"I'm thinking of you, Herman. You and Elizabeth. You and your reputation. The girl's as well, of course, but you are my friend."

Melville smiled and put a hand on Hawthorne's shoulder.
"I fancy her. But I am not a cad. I am not a fool. I have the utmost respect for her, and for Lizzie, and I do appreciate the concern of my dearest friend and mentor. Come."

And on they went, marching up Fifth Avenue.

"I am eager to get this interview over with," Hawthorne said, "and to get on back north."

"Let's take a steamer up the Hudson this time, like I always used to, up to Albany, just the two of us."

"You forget we've left our horses in Amherst, Herman."

"Damn. You're right. Well, maybe we can make arrangements. Anyway my man, you'll be pleased to know that as I stepped off the ship this morning at Fulton Street I resolved then and there to get my adolescent bewitchment behind me."

"All for the best."

They crossed east at Fourteenth Street and then made their way through Union Square Park taking a diagonal route weaving between carriages, horse dung, and massive puddles.

"Nathaniel, have you always stayed on the straight and narrow when it comes to the fairer sex?"

"I've had my share of temptations of course, but yes. I haven't the energy for it, and energy it requires—in vast amounts. After writing a full morning and seeing my family, sharing domestic duties with Sophia—something I have always insisted upon—all I really want to do is either sleep or take a long walk."

Melville found the reply honest—and disheartening—but he chose not to say so. It struck him how a man who could write such a powerful treatise against society's oppressive norms would himself be so freely in step with the very chains and prohibitions he railed against. But then he did say something. He could not help himself.

"What do you think of love?"

"That there are many varieties: brotherly, paternal, maternal . . ."

"I mean romance—romantic love."

"There's that too."

"And how do you feel about it?"

"Now what are *you* driving at?"

"We're so sorry," said Austin, ushering them into the *Salon du The*. "His timing has been uncannily inconvenient for you I realize."

"Perhaps he has been warned as to my melancholic disposition," said Hawthorne only half in jest.

They found a low, round table in a corner with two plush chairs and a U-shaped banquette by a window looking out directly on the park.

"The thing is I can see it perfectly," said Emily. "You'd be a very valued professor."

"And would you move to Amherst?" said Austin.

"I suppose we would, yes. We're moving no matter what befalls. We have outgrown the farmhouse in Lenox, and we have been having difficulties of late with the landlord, and my original thought was to return to Salem, to be near the sea, where I might obtain employment at the Custom House."

"We cannot offer you an ocean view," said Emily, "but I daresay teaching would be a worthier and more satisfying way of spending one's time."

"I apologize for being so forward," Austin continued, "but it is a topic that interests me. Might I infer then that the earnings from your books are not sufficient?"

"We were discussing this very topic over lunch," said Melville, studying Emily's hands. "It is virtually impossible to earn a living with one's pen."

"Really?" questioned Austin.

"The mathematics are dismal. This is not England, or France."

"In any event," said Hawthorne, "it is a dull topic and I'm sure a suitable solution shall present itself and, to put you both at ease, I can assure you that I had already agreed to accompany Herman here to the city where I need to have a chat with my publisher. So, nothing is lost and I am sure to meet up with Squire Dickinson in a not too-distant future."

"I do not find the topic dull in the slightest," said Emily. "On the one hand, women know so little about how to work for remuneration and . . ."

"On the other? . . ." Melville interjected with a sardonic grin.

". . . While *on the other*," she continued, answering his grin with one of her own, "it is a topic that, in general, is often on many people's minds but which they are embarrassed to articulate. Now that I think of it, it is rather similar to . . ."

Here she blushed, for her words had gotten ahead of her.

"Similar to?. . ." asked Melville.

The other two men went silent and took a sudden and almost feverish interest in the tea service menu printed on cards in front of them.

"Similar to the world's hesitation to speak about the complicated territories pertaining to reproduction."

Melville gleamed, admiring her spunk. Lizzie would never have marched on like that, not even in the old days when he first met her. Hawthorne, weighing the probability that all of his friend's assurances offered during their walk might very well have been prime examples of arch hypocrisy, was not pleased.

"Well I do think it a dull topic," he said. "Dull and dreary."

"You may have a point," said Melville. For some reason Emily took this statement of solidarity as a rejection, one that pricked her.

"Then what topics of discussion outshine it? Love and poetry? Politics and history?"

"You find those topics dull, sister?"

"I find them invariably trite and specious and above all self-serving, as a way to show-off or as a way of justifying one's own behavior."

"The 'Trite and Specious'——a fine name for a London Pub," said Melville.

"What would you speak about Mr. Melville?" asked Austin.

"How about conversation itself? Its repetitiveness, its cumbersome, greasy side, proffered up to lubricate the generally awkward and nervous state found in all humans who resort to it when they congregate——as we are."

"What the deuce are you going on about now?" said Hawthorne.

The waiter came and took their orders. Melville chose to ignore his friend's irritation, one that was beginning to irritate him as well.

"If you observe people, be they in a museum regarding a great work of art, be they in a whaling frigate beholding a gam of giant humpbacks, be they on a train or on a steamer, one hears, in ninety-nine percent of the cases, words spoken for their own sake, words spoken to make noise, words

Then, all of a sudden, as if on cue, all four of them looked up and turned their heads in the same direction, taking in a healthy looking thirty-two-year-old man wearing a correct, but somewhat disheveled, suit *sans* cravat.

"How do you do?" said the man. "So sorry for this interruption. My name is Walter Whitman and I write for various publications here in the City. I was wondering, hoping, that you, Mr. Hawthorne, and you, Mr. Melville, might concede to a brief interview."

8

Now I see what there is in a name, a word, liquid, sane,
unruly,
musical, self-sufficient,
I see that the word of my city is that word from old,
Because I see that word nested in nests of water-bays,
superb,
Rich, hemm'd thick all around with sailships and steam-
ships, an
island sixteen miles long,
Numberless crowded streets, high growth of iron, slender,
strong,
light, splendidly uprising toward clear skies.
　　　　　　　　— FROM *MANNAHATTA* BY WALT WHITMAN

CYRUS CLARK AWAKENED TOWARD SEVEN PM NAKED UPON A
bed in a ground floor flat off of Chambers Street. He needed

to get dressed and make his way home before his wife would begin to worry. But he was reluctant to risk bestirring Walt Whitman, still sleeping beside him, who might see fit to renew their tedious argument. The poet, naked as well, slept fitfully, facing the wall, lightly snoring now and then, making it difficult to judge how tightly moored he might be to Morpheus' Landing.

Cyrus admired the broad shoulders, the toughened back muscles, the knobby vertebrae, the two dark warts where a seraphim or a demon's wing might blossom. The rear end, however, was curiously feminine, wide, smooth, pink, hairless. Limiting his vision to just this part of Whitman's anatomy the weight of perversity lightened. With just this perspective, all he has had is a wild roll with another woman as men are wont to do, another woman in the afternoon after work, an adulterous but passionate assignation. What was the difference really? The whole tawdry human mess was but skin and tissue and bestial urges driving one along with only the barest pretense of control or discretion. Or so he told himself, replaying the point of view he attempted to defend against Whitman's belittling sarcasm. But he knew then as the gentle summer evening crept in, with its light both comforting and melancholy and with the taste of sour ale and tobacco on his tongue, that it was sheer specificity that drove him to take such risks. It was the cock and balls between his legs and the cock and balls drooping from the poet's other side that set the fever in play. He had no notion as to why. He only knew it was an animal thing as much a part of him as what it was that drove bucks to lock antlers. The reverends could thunder and rattle all they wished from their termite-infested pulpits but Nature simply smiled and drooled and went about her business.

When making love to his wife, an act he was only per-
suaded to attempt when she made her own inclinations
obvious, his mind went elsewhere. To remain vigorous
with her, he would at first have to imagine other women,
the young girl who sold newspapers up the block from
the press, the bosomy waitress at the pub he frequented
far too often these days, even his wife's twelve-year-old
sister, doing unspeakably vile things to the sweet virginal
creature despite her cries of fear and protest. And then the
inevitable would occur. In order to keep from flagging just
when his wife was most in need, the young girl would suddenly morph into his wife's even younger nephew that he
would begin to abuse as well until caught in *flagranti* by
the boy's miraculously naked father who would then begin
to flog him mercilessly with a soiled gutta-percha whip
before having his way with him. This would faithfully get
the job done, and thus it was that Mrs. Clark was permitted to obtain some satisfaction and bear them, to date, four
healthy offspring.

This had been Whitman's point, that it was not so much
which sex one coupled with, but the one that brought on and
maintained desire, that mysterious factor he had feared since
adolescence and that Whitman pretended to celebrate in
private. All Cyrus knew from experience was that encounters like this afternoon's calmed him and allowed him to
continue his own pretense, sometimes for as long as two to
three months.

Ten minutes later after he had managed to extricate
himself from bed, dress, and get the front door unlatched
Whitman turned to face him, manhood in hand, an image
difficult to ignore.

"I invite you to come along with me this evening as I continue my conversation with Misters Hawthorne and Melville. It's the least I can do for you in exchange for your information."

Cyrus adjusted his spectacles, looking about, nodding, attempting to avoid the languorous onanism in full play before him.

"Impossible. I'm so late now as it is."

"Get on with you then before your hell-cat discovers the true dimensions of your sordid Nature."

He pronounced this last word in French and its comely reverberation accompanied Clark along his hurried hike west to the ferry slip and across the river to Brooklyn where decent families dwelled.

An hour later Melville left his hotel alone and found Walt Whitman standing on the newly paved sidewalk whittling a piece of wood.

"Mr. Whitman, I see you were quite serious about continuing our conversation."

"Indeed."

They shook hands.

"I regret to say Mr. Hawthorne is indisposed."

"Nothing serious I trust."

"He rather over-did it at supper and requires bed rest and a good night's sleep to put him right, I imagine. And I am late for my engagement."

Melville had not anticipated having to put so good a face on things so quickly. He was still feeling inner vibrations of stress and displeasure at what had just transpired between himself and his dear friend. Whitman folded his knife and slipped it into his coat pocket.

"If you don't mind, sir, I shall just accompany you until you arrive at your destination."

"By all means. And there are two. Back to the Everett House to collect the Dickinsons and then south again to a dinner."

Melville, who loved to walk, especially in his native city, nevertheless hailed a carriage due to the hour and after giving the driver his instructions the two men took their seats.

"I am not entirely disappointed to have you alone, Mr. Melville, for I have heard rumors about your new work I would very much enjoy confirming."

"Such as. . ."

"That it is a sea story, once again, something to do with whales and whaling and with a particular whale, in fact, who is its protagonist."

"And what might be the providence of such rumors?"

"A friend of a friend who works at Craighead's printers."

"Ah-hah." He was not pleased.

"Is it true?"

"It is."

"I've also heard it is a whale of a book, in size I mean."

"True as well."

"And is it based on your personal experiences the way your other books have been?"

"I think you could say, one could say, that with each book I write, the influence of my personal experiences becomes more and more diluted. The first two books were almost a diary, the third a hybrid, and this tale is almost entirely a creation of my own imaginings. I did, of course, work on a whaling ship for a time, and I have since done significant research to fill in all manner of gaps that remained after my own education in that world ceased."

"And is the main character really a mammoth fish?"

"I see you are a city man, Mr. Whitman."

"Much less than you. I was born in the wilds of Long Island amidst Indians and deer and the remnants of British warships wrecked along the sandbars. Why do you say that?"

"A nice turn of phrase that: *British warships wrecked along the sandbars.* I say it because a whale is not a fish, but a mammal, in all respects."

"Oh yes. I suppose I did know that."

"And The Whale in question is not the book's protagonist, really—one of them certainly—but not the only one."

Thanks to Cyrus Clark, Whitman had, in fact, already read significant tracts from the manuscript.

"*Moby-Dick* is the creature's name, I believe."

"It is."

"And where might such a strange name, come from?"

"From an actual whale, a huge albino Sperm Whale known as Mocha Dick. Mocha being the name of an island off of Chile where the beast was often sighted—a bull leviathan of prodigious strength whose hide was punctuated with numerous snapped harpoons and who took pleasure in attacking his pursuers."

"I had no idea. Sounds more like a devil than a mammal."

"It is a topic the book explores—to a degree."

"Speaking of devils, what are your thoughts on the gargantuan angry devil of slavery still attacking the moral fiber of our nation?"

"Slavery is a vile, immoral, and counterproductive thing."

"Are you with the abolitionists then?"

"I'm not 'with' anyone—but I am against slavery. What normal person would not be?"

"You see no contradiction in being against slavery and against the abolitionist movement? I should advise you, I too feel the same way."

"I did not say I was 'against' the abolitionist movement. I said I was not 'with' anyone. I am a writer, not a politician or a pamphleteer."

The carriage stopped in front of the Everett House and Melville stepped down and entered the hotel. Whitman remained behind and resolved to not pursue the issue any further—mostly due to the fact that Melville had just said something that had penetrated him profoundly. "A writer, not a politician or a pamphleteer." Then what was he?

Melville, aristocratic and confident, handsome and a risk taker, innately stylish, had cut his family bonds with a vengeance. He had worked as a seaman, a whaler, became a mutineer, a lover of savages. A voracious reader of the classics while sailing the vast Pacific and the perilous South Atlantic, his work reflected all of that. The new whale manuscript would surely become a holy bible of American letters. And what had he done? Drifted from job to job, never too far away from kith and kin, teaching, writing his articles, getting all hot and bothered by each and every political craze to grab the headlines, getting tarred and feathered for fooling around with that boy in Southold, writing sentimental sensationalistic silly novels with which he had hoped to achieve fame and fortune by the collar and on the cheap—works that painfully embarrassed him now sitting in the carriage. Melville imbued the exotic with Yankee austerity and deep naturalistic wisdom with titles such as *Omoo*, and *Typee*, *White Jacket,* and now *The Whale*—each one a steady improvement on the one before it while he had tossed out his "novels," *Richard Parker's Widow* and *The Half-Breed: A Tale of the Western Frontier*, *Franklin Evans*—his maudlin stories, *The Wicked Impulse!*, *Death in the School Room*—Good God! Spending his energies willy-nilly, one day a copy editor, one day president of the Brooklyn Art Union, one day a poet, one day a carpenter, one day a flaming Democrat party man, one day the muckraking reporter, all the while chasing boys hither and thither, and here he was doing all he could to wrest half an hour from two men who have the real thing in their veins and who had no time for him and why should they?

Melville returned with Emily and Austin, who both greeted Whitman with smiles and kindness as they took their places in the carriage. As evening surrounded and descended, they headed back downtown. Whitman was now quite subdued and Melville—sensitive, if only unconsciously, to his change in humor—felt a complimentary tinge of yearning and regret. It was aided and abetted by the effects exerted by the violet July hues taking possession of the atmosphere. He knew, not simply as a poetic concept but as a physical fact felt in that moment anatomically, how it was at that very hour at Arrowhead. And among his loved ones that would be found there, he pictured above all his wife and child, his wife still young and laden with another life miraculously folded within her womb and their little Malcolm who might be sitting on the kitchen floor playing with a scrap of potato peel, innocent and vulnerable, while he, their protector, wiled away his time flirting and strutting about down here in the city so changed from his own youth. Emily looked at him, saw that he had "gone away," and felt a stirring in her breast.

"Where do you hope to publish this interview, Mr. Whitman?" she asked in a gentle tone, leaning forward.

"With a bit of luck, they will take it at the New York Herald and at the Brooklyn Eagle."

"You look much more like a poet to me," said Austin. "More a poet than a journalist."

Whitman smiled at the young man taking an instant shine to him. "As a matter of fact, that is what I mostly do. But of course there's no money in it. So . . ."

"I knew it!" said Austin, slapping his knee theatrically, quite pleased with himself.

"A poet, you say," said Melville, coming about. "An admirable vocation if there ever was one. You must show me some of your verse."

"I'd be pleased to. It is something I need to do more of."

"Do you show your work easily?" Emily asked. "It seems to me poems can be so private."

"Private they may be, but they are written to be read, read by others, in my case certainly, and that experience can be very stimulating."

"Quite right," said Melville.

"Tell me, brother," said Emily, looking to lighten, or at least distract, the somber spirits of the two older men. "What does a poet look like exactly?"

Austin pointed to Whitman. "Like him."

Everyone laughed.

"I mean look at me," he went on, "I look like a banker's son. I exude the opposite of personality. Whereas Mr. Whitman displays a raffish, interesting, bohemian bent."

"And do you think," she went on, "that a necessary condition for one to be a poet?"

"For one to be a real poet? The authentic article? Yes, I do."

Emily looked down at her black skirt and gloves, at her customary appearance, the undertaker's daughter. Then she looked up. "What says you, Mr. Whitman?"

"I disagree. I find it difficult to imagine Mr. John Milton, or Livy, or the oriental masters of verse affecting a particular sartorial slant. I think the persona of the *artiste* is something perhaps that has accompanied the decline of craftsmanship."

"This is a very interesting idea Mr. Whitman," Melville said.

"So then, this look of yours has an element of theater to it?" asked Austin.

"It pains me to admit it, but I daresay it does."

"The decline of craftsmanship," Melville repeated.

"Yes," Whitman said, "I am sure the artisans and even the writers of verse during the Middle Ages and the Renaissance did not consider themselves artists as we now define the term. They had a place and knew it. The artist as hero, as a rebel, as a figure who has stepped to the side of society as it were, is relatively new—or so it seems to me."

Melville noted the Morewood mansion coming into view and moved his toes around within his boots. "This is a conversation that merits continuance. But here we are, arriving at our destination."

"I'm very grateful for the time you have been able to spare me. Please convey to Mr. Hawthorne my regards and wishes for his good health when you see him, and if you find yourself bored or insomniac at your dinner party, I shall be at the Downing Oyster House, probably until it closes."

The carriage came to a halt. Whitman jumped out first so as to lend Emily his hand.

"I have heard of this place," said Melville, impressed with the poet's athleticism. "Where is it exactly?"

"At five Broad Street. It is owned and run by a black man and serves the best oysters in the city to a crowd composed of politicians, businessmen, socialites—and ladies with imagination."

"I take note."

"Ladies with imagination?" asked Emily placing a hand under her throat.

To his associates regaled in velvet smoking jackets at the Reform Club in London, John Rowland Morewood—taking gentlemanly understatement to a new extreme—referred to his Manhattan residence as "our flat in New York." The flat in question was a three-story house of generous proportions with an august limestone facade, filled with fine French furnishings, that had an ample private garden, a reflecting pool stocked with trout, and a live-in staff of eight servants. The staff that evening had been augmented with ten additional people to accommodate the seventeen dinner guests. A table had been constructed and set for the event on the garden's graveled main patio under a white awning.

As Melville and the Dickinsons were shown in, fussed over, and presented, the main focus of activity was taking place in the cavernous living room where champagne was being offered. The Duyckinck brothers and their wives came over immediately to greet Melville and his two guests with goodwill and interest. They saw nothing at all amiss in the explanation as to how they met and came to travel with the authors to the city, and a vigorous conversation was initiated

concerning the merits and virtues of the Massachusetts countryside and of New England small-town life with everyone
expressing only positive views with the exception of Austin
who, rapt in this new found world of urban luxury felt only
shame that evening at his village roots.

Though rarely in need of one, Sarah Morewood had an
ideal motive for that evening's gathering. Thanks to a marriage
made by one of her husband's distant cousins, a Londoner
well placed in the Sherry import business who had betrothed
a Spanish woman of title, the guest of honor was a Spanish
duchess pertaining to that same aristocratic Iberian family,
a thirty-year-old widow of great wealth and beauty called
María Luisa Benavides y Fernández de Córdoba. Concurrent
with his elation at having arrived at a social gathering of the
kind he had always dreamed about, Austin Dickinson found
himself instantly besotted as the duchess was presented to
him. Her English was perfect and annunciated with a Bel-
gravian British air. The young woman's neck was long and
delicate, her cheekbones high, and her green eyes set slightly
farther apart than normal, endowing her with an expression
of perpetual grace. What most beguiled him was her long
blond hair rolled into a stylish bun and pierced with a tor-
toise shell *peineta*. This latter object and a magnificent *Mantón
de Manila* she wore about her otherwise bare shoulders were
the only two concessions offered to her native culture. All
the rest was pure Paris but worn unpretentiously. Austin was
not alone in his state of worship for this exotic creature, but
what did distinguish him almost at the outset of his arrival, to
everyone's surprise and to some gentlemen's annoyance, was
the interest she began to show in him.

Melville, most mindful of the familiarity that existed
between his hosts and almost half of their guests with his wife

and kin, and still wounded by his most recent confrontation with Hawthorne, was on his best behavior. He made a special point of introducing Austin and Emily together at all times and in Emily's presence jokingly encouraged Sarah Morewood to find her a suitable dinner partner.

"Suitable in what way, Herman?"

"Handsome, amusing, well-read, eligible."

"In that order?"

"In that order."

"Miss Dickinson, what have you to say to such a list?"

"Tiz not a bad one, although I think my dear mother and father would prefer his state of eligibility to occupy the first place on it."

"Well said. And why not add 'of independent means'?"

"Why not?"

Emily sensed that the amiable, conspiratorial tone Sarah Morewood was using with her was entirely due to the woman's regard for Melville. The socialite's red hair and blue eyes, her fair skin and enviable *poitrine*, her double strand of pearls and the yards of salmon-hued silk used to fashion her gown all contributed to making Emily feel like the woman's housemaid in comparison.

"What about this 'well-read' part?" she asked, grabbing Emily's forearm as if they were practically sisters. "Does that mean you are well-read yourself?"

"Mr. Melville exaggerates."

"You know very well that I do not," he said. And the way he said it, the tension in his voice reflecting a stratagem of dissimulation put Sarah Morewood ever so subtlety on notice.

A waiter appeared with a tray of champagne flutes filled to the top. They all took one. Sarah clinked her glass with Emily's.

"As Madame Pomadour was famous for saying, 'Champagne is the only wine that enhances a woman's beauty.'"

"Then I shall drink much of it," said Emily.

"Nonsense," said Melville. "Neither of you are in need of any further development in that department."

"What a gallant thing to say Herman—though you are blushing! How divine!"

In an attempt to try to draw attention away from his distress Emily only made things worse.

"Madame Pompadour?"

Sarah looked right at her with a sparkle in her eye. "She was the mistress of Louis the XV of France."

Looking to be meddlesome Sarah sat Emily between Melville and a deaf dowager. The Spanish duchess sat between John Morewood and Austin. After dedicating an obligatory five minutes of boring banter to her, the socially awkward Morewood spent the remainder of the meal talking business and real estate with the older males closest to him. This provided the belle from Andalusia free rein with the son of Amherst.

"I think teaching young unfortunate boys is a fascinating thing to do. It is a noble and charitable act."

"Really?"

"*Absolutamente*. But what do you do for amusement?"

"Amusement is frowned upon in Massachusetts."

She laughed at this, placing one of her hands upon his forearm as she did so.

"But, you do not share this point of view, do you?"

"You don't think so?"

"Oh no. I can tell. You put up a good and proper facade, but inside, and when you can, the real you is quite different."

"How can you tell?"

"Because I am like this as well. I recognized a kindred spirit the second you walked in the door."

"Kindred spirit—a duchess from Spain and a humble school teacher from New England?"

"What difference does that make? Six generations ago my family were herding sheep. Besides, I have come to your country to escape all of the pomp and circumstance I grew up with—I am looking for new experiences in a new world."

"What sort of experiences?"

Their eyes locked. The not unpleasant tension between them was relieved only when she looked down and smiled.

True to her word Emily did imbibe a more than healthy quantity of champagne. Virtually everyone around her did. And now they were drinking a burgundy to accompany lamb stew. All of it was contributing to a general erosion of inhibition and Melville felt less and less inclined to maintain his guard. He leaned over to her and spoke in a whisper.

"I cannot stop thinking about this morning . . . on the steamer."

Her eyes widened and with her head she gestured toward the woman seated next to her. "Mr. Melville."

"Don't worry about her. Mrs. Vanderhoven is as deaf as a post. And please call me Herman."

"I shall call you 'Armando,' seeing as how I am soon to have someone called 'Maria Luisa' for a sister-in-law."

"Did you hear what I said?"

"Of course. But tell me something. Is Mr. Hawthorne really indisposed—or is it something else?"

"Something else of course."

"I can only imagine what he may have said to you."

"I wish you wouldn't."

"Have you considered that perhaps he is in the right?"

"I have considered nothing else. I go over and over it all, considering 'everyone,' but my heart, for better or worse, is as attentive to it as Mrs. Vanderhoven's ear."

"Oh dear."

"I would never compromise you."

She looked into his eyes, as if searching for something, "Quote me something else from your whale book. You've no idea how much I yearn to read it."

He swallowed his happiness, gave it a thought, and cleared his throat. "There are certain queer times and occasions in this strange and mixed affair we call life when a man takes this whole universe for a vast practical joke, though the wit thereof he but dimly discerns, and more than suspects that the joke is at nobody's expense but his own."

"Are you engaged to anyone?" the duchess asked Austin.

"In a manner of speaking," he replied, finishing his wine and feeling himself to be perhaps the most cosmopolitan and sophisticated swain within a thousand miles.

"I shall take that as a 'no.' You are not in love with her *ne c'est pa*? Is there someone else?"

"In a manner of speaking."

"I shall take that as a 'yes'! This is the one you feel things for. Do tell. And you are forbidden to answer 'in a manner of speaking'—a most absurd expression."

"Yes, there is someone else. But she is inappropriate . . . for my family."

"What did I tell you—we are kindred spirits. What is 'wrong' with her? Is she black?"

"No!"
"An Indian Squaw?"
"No.
"Is she a he?"
"No!"
"Then?"
"She's Irish."

"How would you describe the joke made at your expense?" asked Emily, beginning to entertain some doubt as to whether she would be to stand properly once the desserts were cleared. She took one last sip of the Sauterne, a wine theretofore unknown to her and which she found sublime.

"Apart from life itself?. . ." Out of habit Melville checked his beard for debris and shot a glance over at Sarah who had spent a good deal of the dinner finding excuses to lean forward in his direction revealing the inviting valley between her breasts. It occurred to him that perhaps her possible encouragement of his dalliance had a hidden motive. Then he looked down toward the table's other extreme where to his continuing astonishment Austin Dickinson still dominated the attentions of the Iberian aristocrat who's beauty he could admire but for whom he felt only negligible attraction. But observing her did dislodge the memory that his father had once visited Spain, before he ever met his mother. And once again he concurred with himself that our fathers are mysteries "as I shall be for Malcolm." It seemed to be a rule of nature. ". . . As you can see Emily I am waxing profound tonight, profundity being another word in this instance for blathering."

"Not at all. I could listen to you blather for a very long time, Armando."

When the guests and their hosts retired to the library for coffees and liqueurs while the servants removed the last plates from the dinner table, Maria Luisa and Austin repaired to a stone bench placed by the reflecting pool. Some of the trout, sensing their proximity, stirred and Austin could almost feel their pent up energy in the dark shallow water.

"You cannot marry a woman you do not love, Austin, a woman you have no desire for. I had a marriage like that and wasted almost ten precious years of my life."

"It is not that simple."

"That is how it seems to you now—but yes it is that simple."

"I am not sure if I wish to marry Fiona either."

"You must break off both engagements and come to Europe for at least a year."

"And what shall I live on?"

"You can live with me—in London and in Paris and in Madrid. You will be my dear cousin, or my tutor, that way I can pay you to help me with my English and the sciences and I shall introduce you to the most fascinating young women on the continent."

"You must not jest with a poor boy from Massachusetts."

"I love that word."

"Which?"

"Mass-a-chu-setts. And my offer is entirely serious. I am so very bored now that I am a widow—bored and relieved—and I just know we would amuse each other to no end."

"I do not know what to say madam."

"*Yes* will do. I sail tomorrow but I shall give you my card before this evening ends so that you can write to me to say when you are arriving."

"Arriving where?"

"London. I shall be there until the end of September."

"You astonish me."

"Promise me you will."

"Dear woman . . ."

Austin came into the library and approached Emily in an altered state. He did his best to ignore the many stares aimed his way as he corralled his sister into a private corner and got straight to the point. "Don't say anything. And please don't ask any questions. Just listen." He then proceeded to relate the extraordinary offer the duchess had made to him. When she reacted as anyone might, his face reddened and he exclaimed, "It is fate, Emily, my fate, this trip to New York, this dinner, walking into this house this evening and meeting this person. It is a once in a lifetime opportunity."

"What about Sue? What about Fiona?"

"I have already made up my mind to return home tomorrow, by way of Fall River, and I shall speak to both of them, freeing them of any compromise of any sort."

"Are you sure Austin? I know how you can be sometimes."

"I have never been so sure of anything in my entire life."

Shortly thereafter Maria Luisa gave her card to Austin and then said goodnight to all, begging their pardon and proffering the legitimate excuse of an early departure the following day. As Austin lingered behind to have a few more words with his new patroness, Melville and Emily went about making their farewells to the Morewoods, Melville feigning an obligation to see the siblings back to their hotel. The communal level of inebriation was such that no one seemed to notice.

Waiting for their carriage out front, and for Austin to appear, Emily told Melville what had happened. She was fighting tears.

He spoke her name. He said it with tenderness. She tuned to face him. "I cannot believe it."

"He'll be fine."

She looked off to the side, not yet willing to admit his opinion.

"These things happen to young men."

"These *things*."

"Adventures. They all add up and impart character over time. The only unusual thing in this instance is that you, his sister, are bearing witness to it."

"There is nothing 'usual' about that most singular woman."

"On that point I am in agreement. But he will be fine. I'm sure of it. Who knows if he shall actually follow through with it? When I left home, for a much longer period of time, enmeshed in an enterprise far more perilous, no one from my family was there to see it."

"I wish I had never left Amherst. That we had both stayed behind."

"Do you really?"

She turned away from him once more. He stood there by the carriage, its driver still awaiting direction. The horse stamped its right front hoof upon the hardened earth of the deserted street.

"It has been a long day," he said.

"I am not in the least bit tired," she said. "I suppose it must be the coffee after all that wine."

"All right," he said. ". . . Well . . . There is always the Oyster House that fellow Whitman mentioned. It's close by."

"Yes," she said, shrugging her girlish shoulders, "Why not? In for a penny . . . Let me go back in and see what's keeping him."

Some minutes later the three of them entered the establishment. Numerous carriages were parked out front and a golden light given off from a score of crystal chandeliers gave the place an inviting glow. A long bar ran down one side, a large section of which was reserved for waiters shucking hills of oysters. Behind them was a line of mirrors, baskets of lemons, and damp crates filled with finely chiseled ice. The rest of the room was a sea of round tables and booths packed at that hour with a decidedly wealthy and successful looking clientele.

"How extraordinary," said Emily. Her spirits seemed to rise the instant they came in through heavy doors of leaded beveled glass. Austin, feeling almost sinful for merely being there, took in the magical aura of the space and claimed it as yet another sign of how his life must change.

"Welcome to New York," said Melville, relieved to see Emily smile again and feeling a glimmer of gratuitous pride about his native town that had such cosmopolitan eateries hidden about and going full tilt at such an hour.

They found Whitman at a corner table near the kitchen conspiring with a serious looking, well-attired black man approximately Whitman and Melville's age. This gentleman, who was facing the establishment's entrance, rose as he realized Melville and the Dickinsons were headed to the table. Whitman turned around and then stood just as they arrived.

"Mr. Whitman," Melville said.

"Mr. Melville, Mister Dickinson, Miss Dickinson. What a pleasant surprise. I did not think for a minute you might actually consider my invitation."

"Our dinner party has put us into a bit of a state and we decided that we were in need of a change of air before retiring."

"You have come to the right address. May I present Mr. Thomas Downing whose father owns this fine saloon. Thomas, this is Herman Melville, Miss Emily Dickinson, and her brother Austin."

Downing shook hands with the two men and made to kiss Emily's saying, "Enchanté."

She had never met a gentleman of color before.

"How do you do?"

"I don't actually speak French but I find a few random phrases impress the ladies."

"Most impressive," she said, blushing.

"Are you Melville the writer, sir?"

"I am."

"I am a devoted reader of your books."

"I am very pleased to learn that, Mr. Downing."

"The first two dozen oysters and a bottle of French white wine I highly recommend are on the house."

"That's very kind. Thank you."

"I must continue to circulate." Then, turning to Whitman, "You won't forget our chat, Walter."

"How could I?"

Just as Thomas Downing was taking his leave, the kitchen doors opened and his father, the distinguished proprietor, George Downing, appeared. Introductions were repeated all around. Melville noticed how the elder man offered a particularly warm handshake to Whitman.

"I would be very pleased to stay and converse with such an artistic circle, but I need to go. We don't get enough of your kind in here and the place is in need of you. Although I shouldn't complain too much because my normal clientele keeps things profitable."

"What sort of people are they?" asked Emily. The answer to this question had already been provided by Whitman hours earlier but she was so entranced with the elder Mr. Downing's sonorous voice and exquisite manner that she wished to try to prolong his presence there.

"Lots of politicians, mostly the corrupt ones who've got all our money! And men of business, 'entrepreneurs' as some of them like to be called, whose intake of spirits is in direct proportion to their profound boredom with what it is they do all day."

"Good gracious."

"I must be on my way. I row out each night at this hour to meet the dredging skipjacks before they reach and unload at the barges, to make sure we only obtain the very best they have."

"You row out into the harbor at night sir?" Austin asked him.

"A strong young man does the rowing now, like Thomas here used to once upon a time."

"I am mightily impressed," Austin replied.

"As a boy," Melville said for the second time that day, reiterated now for Emily's benefit, "I would dive for them off Whitehall Slip. The river was clear and clean then."

"I'll be. Thomas, make sure this man and this table's orders go on the house!"

"I've already invited them, father."

The oysters and two bottles of Muscadet arrived in less than a minute.

"When are you all returning to the North Country?" asked Whitman serving the wine.

"Sometime tomorrow or the next day I expect, no, Emily?"

"Yes. Tomorrow would be better. I'd worry less about getting back on time."

"Tomorrow it is then. I'm not sure what Nathaniel's plans will be."

"I'd like to make a suggestion if you don't mind," said Whitman.

"Not at all."

"Rather than take the steamship again, why not try a new route provided by the Long Island Railroad. Have you done that yet?"

"No sir. I usually go up the Hudson, or go by train to Albany, which is considerably closer to home than Boston."

"I strongly recommend it, especially if you have never seen Long Island, Miss Dickinson. One leaves from Brooklyn and goes all the way out to Greenport on the North Fork, which is a swell place to picnic this time of year. And from there, a steamer ferry takes you to New London, Connecticut, where there are trains to Boston, and perhaps to other Massachusetts towns as well."

"Actually, New London does have good transport to Amherst and Northampton, I believe. What do you think, Emily? Do you have any special interest in passing through Fall River again?"

"I do not. But I believe Austin does."

"I have to catch the very first steamer back to Fall River at dawn tomorrow, in a matter of hours from now."

Melville could judge by his tone and demeanor that the boy's mind was unmovable, and he began to turn down

Whitman's suggestion, but then Austin intervened. "But Emily is in good hands with you gentlemen, and we could meet in North Hadley the day after tomorrow, so that she and I might arrive home together."

Emily's first instinct was to protest and to insist that they travel together, if only for decorum's sake, but, in an instant, reading his face that she knew so well, she saw that he preferred to go alone—that the prospect she be taken off his hands was for him a distinctive advantage. And so she said, "We could do that. I shall be in no shape tomorrow to rise at dawn."

Melville dispatched an additional pair of oysters. Though fascinated by his brutish technique of slurping them down directly from the shell, she continued to follow a daintier approach aided by a small fork, the likes of which she had never seen.

"Well that's settled then," said Melville, hoping to hide the satisfaction he felt, wiping his lips with a broad white napkin. "I'm always available to try something new."

"This wine *is* good," said Whitman, pleased his suggestion had been accepted.

"Very good," said Emily. "Though it is the last thing I need now."

"Have you ever been to France, Miss Dickinson?"

"Not only have I not been to France, Mr. Whitman, this is the first time I have left Massachusetts."

"Good grief!"

"I expect that makes me a lady *sans* imagination in your eyes."

"*Touché!*"

The conversation about craftsmanship and the evolving definition of art and artists that had been interrupted by the dinner party was rejoined and a fine time was had by all. But the high point for Emily in this labyrinthine day filled with agitation and novel sensations—with the exception of the pre-dawn kiss—came when the restaurant's piano player, a thin black man in evening attire, approached their table to see if they had any special requests. The question, put kindly, was met at first with a polite and awkward silence until Emily meekly said, "Are you familiar with the sonatas of Johann Sebastian Bach?"

The musician, who spent his professional life banging out Stephen Foster tunes and songs with titles such as "Molly Do You Love Me?" and "Nelly Bly," looked at the thin, somberly dressed girl with particular interest.

"Why yes, madam, I am. They were written, however, for the violin and the flute. But if you'd like, I can try my hands at one of the Goldberg Variations he wrote for the harpsichord. It's so late now, my normal clients won't even notice."

"I'd like that very much."

But notice they did, and it was at this hour that Melville, watching Emily as she responded to the music, sensed himself ascending into another sphere, one in which his own writing felt stale, one in which the only thing that mattered was being able to watch her eyes. As the pianist played a careful and heartfelt version of the *Canon of the Fifth*, a silence gradually took hold of the restaurant, bar, and kitchens until, toward the end, the only extraneous sound heard was the occasional cough. When he finished the room broke out in raucous applause coinciding with Melville and Emily and Austin's departure. The pianist gave her a respectful nod and a smile that she returned in kind.

William Johnson heard the impromptu Bach recital as well. From his hiding place in a ventilated corner of the basement between stacked oyster barrels broken and unused for a decade he took the remarkable change of noise above—from a ribald revelry so constant he had almost become numb to it, into an ecclesiastical state of musical grace—as a positive omen blessing his departure scheduled for the following day. Born on a plantation in Carolina, a grandchild to a man from the banks of the Gambia River and a Chickasaw squaw, he had been on the move for a month. He had passed from safe house to safe house until taken under George Downing's wing three days earlier. They had fed him well, but the strong briny odor that clung to him closed up in the dark coolness where two fat calico cats waged war on intrusive vermin had proved difficult. He had yet to try on the new clothes Downing's son had brought him yesterday. They remained folded next to his Bible and his treasured copy of a Canadian textbook of geography that espoused the "natural theology" of William Paley. Johnson enjoyed impressing white folk with one of the book's key phrases: Everywhere in Nature there is design and there cannot be design without a designer. The book had been a gift from his master's wife, a kindly woman exquisitely adept at turning a blind eye to her husband's penchant for perversity.

There were times when he was homesick for the plantation, for his friends there, the cornbread, the chicory brew, even for the sex he had with Master Mitchell. But the recollection of the young foreman's envy, insults, and whippings, and the constant drudge of the work, could be relied upon to toss a bucket of water on such nostalgic embers.

Arriving under the cover of night, he had seen very little of New York. What most impressed him was that a man of his own race, Mr. Downing, had risen here to become the owner of a profitable business and that his son had gone to college. If he could just achieve a quarter of that before he died he would consider his life to have been a fine and wondrous thing. The Lord God Almighty clearly helped those who helped themselves, and tomorrow's journey would be his last, getting him to where he could try to live as a free man.

The geography book was his compass. Just following strangers about and hiding, never knowing where he was or to where he was going, save for the names white men had assigned to the land and the rivers and towns, and knowing his route to be generally north, all produced a vertigo the book becalmed. He was learning the nature of the rocks and the sediments and the families of the trees. And now this music, like none he had ever listened to. God was good— yes, sir—God was good. And may God bless my mama, he prayed, and guide her gently away from the troubled fields darkly sowed by Satan's ungrateful angels and guide her up the mountain at a pace that shall not tire her and lead her God into the luminous carefree pastures hidden there above.

George Downing never tired of watching the southern tip of Manhattan recede at night as the skiff made its way out toward the straight of Giovanni Verrazanno. The ships moored about the Battery, the flickering lights of the low dwellings, the summer river smell of ripening silts and drifting blossoms. His wife was fast asleep back there and his son up to God knows what, and that new boy in the basement, too handsome and too smooth he feared to avoid coming to a bad end in these northern cities. His nephew rowed well, was the best at it so far, long clean strokes that barely caused the oarlocks to creak.

"What do you think about boy as you pull those oars?"

"I just count, sir."

"Count."

"Yes, sir. One-two . . . then . . . three-four. Like that."

"And your mind does not wander?"

"During the counting? Maybe it does—long as you're here making sure I don't row into something. What is it you think about, sir?"

"About numbers as well, now that I consider it. What prices I think I can get away with. What I'm willing to spend if my more reliable oystermen tell me it's worth it."

"But you've been at this for years now."

"That I have."

"You must know pretty much about all those numbers."

"I guess I do."

"So what do you really think about?"

"Seems to me I was the one who asked *you* that question."

"I'll tell you if you tell me."

Downing smiled at the boy's pluck. Sometimes this son of his sister reminded him of what he had been like more than his own son did. Happens in many families he supposed.

"You have yourself a deal, boy."

The boy did not pause in his rowing. The grace he employed did not alter. A mainsail and a jib would not have moved them along the water any faster.

"I think about all kinds of things. I think about women mostly. And I think about how long it would take me to row this thing up to where the river gets born. I think about rowing to France. I think about having a house up by the Palisades where I could fish and grow my own vegetables and have a cute wife. I go over all the details in bits and pieces."

"That is a good and honest list, though I don't recommend you try rowing to France, at least not in any skiff of mine."

"Yes, sir. Now, it's your turn."

"Hmmm. Let's see. I think a lot about how this city was when I first came to it and how it has changed. I worry about all of the injustice that continues to hold sway. Every time I think something good happens, I see something else that reminds me how steep and slippery the road is. I think about new recipes. I think about Sergius Orata, the first oysterman of the Roman Republic. I contemplate the wonders of *crassostrea virginica*. I worry about my son. I even worry about you and your sisters and your mother. I think about this earth we're on and the oceans and the continents and how the Lord keeps it all moving no matter how mean or vile his servants behave themselves. That's about it, I reckon."

"So you don't think about women no more."

Downing laughed easily up into the damp evening air.

Melville and the young Dickinsons were silent during the first half of their carriage ride uptown. He fought a powerful urge to embrace her, to kiss her again, to drag her into an empty room and lock the door. But the closest he came to any physical contact with her was to place his hand down on the seat between them, inches away from hers while Austin, already living in the future, looked out upon the empty city streets. Melville tortured himself about whether he should try to move his hand a bit closer in the hope she might allow him to come in contact with her fingers.

She realized she was inebriated, more so than she had ever been. It was not unpleasant, and she sat there relaxed, going over the day, trying to keep her eyes open, feeling safe in the dark, vast city for having Melville next to her and her brother seated across from her. She wondered how her mother and Lavinia and her father were faring, all of them separated by such wide distances.

Melville fixed his gaze on the three-quarter moon as they went along the east side of Washington Square and wondered about the night itself. He thought that, like the moon, it was one of those simple things that revealed realities of tremendous proportions. The reason the night arrived at all and then went away was that the world he experienced—where things were anchored to the Earth by gravity and where life took place looking ahead or behind, up or down—was in fact a massive sphere, a planet that turned in space as it revolved in kind around the Sun. It was a simple, vertiginous fact people rarely considered so disheartening were the implications and so contrary to one's sense of the quotidian. How could a globe so large move through space so quickly while leaving the oceans and the trees and the creatures upon it so stable, so in place? A whale swimming by a ship, diving deep down through the sea, glimpsed straight ahead for a second, was in fact on its side upon the spinning world and the sea with it and yet none of it fell away and all of it was experienced as if the sky remained above and the firmament below.

"I've had a lovely evening, Herman," she said all of a sudden.

"And I."

"And what a magical place that oyster den, and what a magical thing it was that happened."

"It happened because of you. I am sure it was and shall remain a singular event."

"You've been so kind to us."

He saw them to the front desk and woke up the night man who put room keys in their hands.

"Have a safe journey, Austin. We will see you in North Hadley."

"Goodnight, Mr. Melville."

The men shook hands and Austin kissed his sister good-bye and began to climb the stairs exhausted and resolute. Melville turned to Emily.

"Get a good night's sleep, or as much as you can. I'll come by tomorrow to get you around eight a.m."

She lowered her head in gratitude for his discretion, clasping the key with both hands, and then she looked at him again.

"I shall never forget this morning," she said in a whisper.

"Nor I."

Dear Sophia,

I am returning home tomorrow, Wednesday, and with any good fortune may arrive to you before this brief missive. Nevertheless, it does me good to put down some thoughts and impressions. I wrote a note earlier this evening to Melville informing him of my plans, then fell asleep until now.

I regret to report my journey has been riddled with disappointment. Since I last wrote to you, what appeared to be a situation getting out of hand has only worsened in my opinion. I expect it will please you to some degree as I tell you your opinion regarding out talented neighbor now seems a more accurate one than mine had been. Perhaps it is just that he is younger than I—surely that has something to do with it—but there are questions of character as well and as we know from Heraclitus "a man's character is his fate."

I will not sully this page with gossip for I still consider him a formidable writer and, yes, a friend. But we are indeed very different, and suffice it to say, I have never missed my dear sweet wife and our three special children as much as I have these past twenty-four hours. My only thoughts now are to return to you all posthaste. Though my only true desire has been to stay with you, to be a worthy husband and father, to continue my work, and to do all I can to bring about a more suitable living arrangement for us all, I feel it now with special urgency and resolve. So, though I have not succeeded in meeting with Mr. Dickinson, one could say that this strange, uneven, and stressful trip has been beneficial.

In any event, it is late and I must blow out the candle and go back to sleep so that I might steal away from this far too populous, agitated, and disturbing city as swiftly as I can upon the morn.

Your loving, N

9

To HIS SURPRISE AND DISCOMFORT, AUSTIN DICKINSON discovered that Nathaniel Hawthorne was a fellow passenger aboard the steamship *Priscilla*. Disinclined to explain his solitary presence, especially at so early an hour, and not at all disposed toward having to make further conversation with the esteemed author, he devoted an inordinate amount of his depleted energy aboard ship avoiding contact with the man. That Hawthorne was traveling alone also pricked his conscience. Surely, Herman Melville was a man of character, he tried to tell himself—though to what extent any man's character was reliable when women were concerned, using himself as an example, remained in doubt. He did, he hoped, also understand that Walter Whitman would also be accompanying his sister and Melville.

Emily found Whitman's handsome dark friend painfully shy. His presence imbued the train compartment with a faint scent of fish and lemons. Melville noticed the young man's gnarled, calloused farmhand fingers, the new clothes that did not fit well plus the worn boots and drew a reasonable conclusion. Whitman's query put to him the evening before regarding the abolitionists acquired new resonance. His first reaction was irritation at the notion they had been taken advantage of, that they were being used as cover to help an escaped slave flee North. He fumed to himself, feigning righteousness as Emily and Whitman and William Johnson made small talk, that if only Whitman had just asked him about it honestly they would have surely acceded. That Whitman had felt the need to lie was insulting. And what if something should go wrong? There were Blackbirders lurking about at all the major stations hoping to make an arrest and claim their bounty. How would that make him look? What would Mr. Dickinson say about the New York author who got his daughter involved in an illegal transaction? The fury within him grew and he was on the verge of interrupting the others to ask Whitman to step out into the corridor so that he might vent his anger appropriately. But precisely for that reason, he began to pay attention to the others more closely.

William Johnson sat there with them, awkward but in possession of his dignity, in that compartment with three New Englanders who, for however aware they were inside of the situation's novelty, went out of their way externally to put the young man at ease. Would he really have said yes if Whitman had been truthful? Or might he have evinced compassion and empathy while coming up with an excuse to return north with Emily by another route? When Whitman had asked him his views on abolition, he had struck a pose of aloofness from worldly, local politics, claiming some special allegiance to an artistic dedication that somehow transcended mundane issues. He who was getting closer with each week to publishing a book with the character of Queequeg in it. He who has spent months living, sleeping, and having relations with natives in the Pacific. He whose grandfather had been an instigator at the Boston Tea Party. And yet he knew, in a quiet, ugly, private place within he would be pleased to seal, that he would indeed have said no to Whitman. He felt ashamed. This was not a newspaper quarrel carried out in print, nor a gentlemanly debate heating up after dinner drinks at a club, but an actual human being sitting there among them who in all likelihood had been born into and brought up within the institution of human slavery. And if he were to be completely honest, he would have to recognize as well that he was grateful for their company. Intuition advised him that being alone with emily during the journey back, even in the company of her brother, under the censorious shadow cast by Hawthorne's absence, his chances for—for what?—for wooing her more successfully— would be severely diminished. Such a degree of forced intimacy at that juncture would be more likely to drive her away. Having company about, a foil and a distraction they might both respond to, would help keep the flame lit between them.

Eventually Whitman and Melville fell asleep, leaving Emily and William Johnson awake. Both of them were entranced by the fine views passing by out the large window.

"Where are you from, Mr. Johnson?"

"I was born—on a—farm—near a small town called Ashville, Miss, a day's ride south from Charlestown, South Carolina."

"A dear friend of mine from Boston moved to the South, to Louisiana, I believe, but I have not any southern acquaintances and, I have to say, I find the manner of speaking very charming."

"There's folks who speak a spell better than I, Miss. I grew up working—on the farm—and I have not had the advantage of book learnin'."

"Nevertheless, it gives me pleasure to hear you speak."

"I do read. My mama taught me to read by teaching me the Bible."

"That is how I learned as well—I think. I can barely remember. But both my parents are serious readers of the Scriptures and we were made to read them, and recite them, well, religiously. Mr. Melville here is a writer of books."

"That I have been told. Mr. Whitman, too."

"So, we fellow readers are in excellent company!"

Between the Hyde Park and Suffolk stations, the views were of pastures and horse farms and rolling leas with nary a hint of the vast salt waters of the nearby sound. One particular view, just past Westbury, of a gentle wooded rise with clearings where wild flowers grew in profusion, inspired William Johnson to proclaim, "The hills—from whence cometh my help."

Emily, smiling, replied, "My help cometh from the Lord, which made heaven and earth."

"Oh my, Miss Emily."

"Psalm number one-twenty-one. I know it well."

"Mightily impressed I am. Do you believe in the Bible, Miss Emily?"

"In what sense?"

"In every sense, I guess."

"My facile answer, the one I would give in public, the one I would say when seated at my parents' table, would be yes,"

"Now that is a wise answer, wise and sly and incomplete."

"Cowardly and incomplete perhaps," she said. And this comment of hers inspired him anew.

"They were cowards to God's Covenant, refused to walk by his Word. They forgot what he had done—the marvels he'd done right before their eyes."

Melville, awake now and listening but with his eyes still closed, startled them both with a quote of his own . . . "No more masses and corpse gifts—no more tithes and offerings to make men poor—no more prayers or psalms to make men cowards—no more christenings and penances and confessions and marriages."

"What heresy is that, Mr. Melville?" Johnson asked.

"Some lines from the heretical Walter Scott," he answered, opening his eyes and looking at Emily.

"And yet you have married," Emily said to him with a mischievous grin.

"Now I shall quote Saint Ambrose, 'If you are in Rome, live in the Roman way; if you are elsewhere, live as they do there.'"

"I see," she said. "An adage you have taken fullest to the heart."

"Who was this Walter Scott? And I am ashamed to add I have never heard of Saint Ambrose neither," Johnson said, wide-eyed.

"Scott was a Scot. As for the other fellow, I've no idea."

"The only thing I know about St. Ambrose," said Emily, "is that he is the patron saint of bee keepers."

"Hmm," said Whitman, awake now as well, "Honey is a bee's nectar. There must be some relation to the word

125

ambrosia, a drink, a nectar that conferred permanent youth and immortality, brought, it was said, by doves to the gods on Mount Olympus."

"Immortality, as in not dying?" asked Johnson.

"Exactly that," said Melville.

"As you can see, William," Whitman added, touching the man on his knee for emphasis, "you are no longer in Bible class but in the wicked North."

"I would not care to be immortal," said Emily.

"How about ageless?" Melville asked. "How about if you could remain the age you are right now?"

"I should think I would get bored with it. I think it is through the process of ageing, that it is because of our mortality, that one appreciates what one has, that one feels things at all, in the moment."

"I agree," said Melville. "I certainly appreciate the present more, knowing what, inevitably, is going to come."

They locked eyes again.

"I am all for immortality and not growing old," said Whitman. "I am in a state of health and life now that I should like to conserve forever. God's design to have instructed Nature to make all living things age and die is as cruel as cruel can be."

"The Lord giveth, and the Lord taketh away," said Johnson.

Between Medford and Riverhead the terrain was dull. Acres of scrub oak and shabby pine devoid of grace or majesty, a desert of low sparse growth Emily hoped would not continue for very long. And then, at Jamesport, everything did change. What had been low, sharp and prickly softened again with the appearance of tended lawns, leafy trees, and the shimmering waters of Flanders Bay. Moored skiffs, sailboats, bright sand, and white gulls resting on the sloping shingled roofs of modest white clapboard houses. Here the break from the city was complete, the sensation that Manhattan had been left definitively behind was palpable.

"Look, Armando—It's lovely."

She said it innocently, spontaneously. No longer was he Mr. Melville. The tenderness of this simple gesture harpooned his heart. And Whitman, a clumsy man physically at times but, a sensitive one in every other regard, picked up on it. What he had sensed the day and night before, and then seeing how their travel party had suddenly dwindled from four of them to just these two, underlined it further. The scandal of it appealed to him, in a genuine and nonjudgmental way. He took it as a healthy sign of Nature when beings were attracted to each other despite society's restrictions. He knew Melville was married to the daughter of a well-known Boston judge, but the man had his reputation as well. Anyone capable of cavorting for months with primitive peoples on an island on the other side of the Earth in no apparent hurry to return to civilization would surely not feel overly bound by a New England marriage vow. The girl's situation was something else again. She appeared to be unblemished and a New Englander through and through who had clearly been raised within a family of upright Puritans. The plain way she dressed and wore her hair and carried herself all bespoke decorum.

The train arrived at Greenport half an hour later where the foursome hired a carriage to take them to the picnic grounds from where one could see the ferry piers. The only black man William Johnson saw in that extremity of Long

Island that day was the gentleman who drove the carriage, a man who looked at Johnson with alternating measures of skepticism and astonishment.

When they arrived at their destination, a park with tall trees and a small pond that ended at a beach, the driver spoke to Whitman, who had offered to pay, as the others walked off.

"S'cuse me sir—one minute."

Whitman put his change back into his pocket and smiled at the man.

"I'm usually very good at minding my own business, sir, but you all seem like good folk and I'd hate to see something sour happen."

"Go on."

"The colored man with you. He a slave?"

"What are you getting at man?"

"What I'm getting at is that you can count the number of colored folk around here on one hand and all of them are known and accounted for—so this man you have with you is going to draw a lot of attention as you try to get on that ferry. If you can't give a proper explanation for him you are going to have some trouble on your hands and that poor boy will go back to where he come from. This is not a community in sympathy with the abolitionist movement."

"I see."

"I just thought you should know."

"Well, I do appreciate that."

"Perhaps you were told differently—but I have seen bad things happen here of this nature."

"What is your own story, if you don't mind my asking?"

"All the coloreds in this area, all five of us, are related and related in kind to the Shinnecock Indians who were here before everyone else. One of them married a black woman some time ago. Nobody knows where she came from."

Our friend William Johnson, here, also has an American Indian ancestor, but it has not done him any good."

"Because he comes from the South."

"Yes."

"There you go then. We live on a reservation. They can't do us any harm there."

"No way you could pass our man off as I relative I suppose."

"Not with that accent of his. And moving him around in broad daylight is not the best plan either, I can tell you that."

This irked Whitman to no end because part of him had known it to be true and he had been warned against it by others and he had gone ahead anyway, forcing himself to believe it all the imaginings of alarmists. His own benevolent and progressive views of New York and Long Island—in spite of his own harrowing experience in the township of Southold, an event he had deposited in a different archive—had gotten in his way.

"What would you suggest?" he asked, suddenly solicitous of a man who, up until ten minutes ago, was barely worth regarding.

"Either wait until nightfall and go for the last ferry taking your chances when the Blackbirders are mostly in the taverns getting drunk—or—go back and get him up to Boston the way he's supposed to go."

Whitman looked down, perturbed. By this time, the others had stopped and turned in their tracks. Shielding their eyes from the glaring sun they were aware something was afoot. He could not face them with this bleak revelation. But should he risk having Johnson apprehended that afternoon? The shame of it, and the publicity when the local press got wind of it, would be excruciating. His pause and paralysis allowed the carriage driver's brain to pursue another option.

"Or . . ."

Whitman looked up.

" . . . I had a client this morning, a local man of good standing I overheard worrying about how to get his sailboat to New London for repairs, looking for someone to get it there for him."

"Could you look into that for us? I'll make it worth your while."

"I could do that. He doesn't live far from here. But do you know how to sail?"

"One of us certainly does. Look, we'll be just over there under that tree," said Whitman pointing to a spot near the beach.

As the driver pulled away Melville came up to Whitman.

"What was that all about?"

"We have to talk, I'm afraid."

"Let me offer a guess—something about this escaped slave you're looking to get up to Boston."

Whitman, sheepish, scratched the back of his neck.

"Did he say something?"

"Nope."

"I suppose it has been somewhat obvious."

"I don't think Emily suspects, but why would she?"

"I'm sorry I didn't come on straight to you about it."

"Me, too."

"And now we—I—have a problem."

As they started to walk to join Emily and Johnson who had resumed strolling toward the beach on their own, Whitman related his conversation with the driver.

"What kind of a boat is it?"

"I've no idea. I don't know anything about boats. But look, if worse comes to worse I'll invent some kind of excuse and take William back to New York with me on the train this afternoon and try again tomorrow going north by the usual route. You and Miss Dickinson can take the ferry as planned. I don't know what I was thinking."

"Let's see what transpires," said Melville, patting Whitman on the back. "I must say the idea a man can't go where he wishes in this country, any man who is not a criminal convicted of an actual crime, makes me angry."

"I'd hoped we were sufficiently far north to be rid of these other kinds of people. I mean, this is the State of New York."

"I'm sure in ten years time no one young today will believe these things ever went on. But at the moment, we are still in the middle of it. It's painful to think about but I expect we need to. I feel bad too about flying high over your question yesterday about the abolitionists. It's just that my natural reaction when faced with fanatics of any stripe is to turn and run!"

Whitman laughed, relieved by this change in Melville's humor. Alienating such a talent was not something he had looked forward to.

While the carriage driver ran his errand the four travelers rested under an elm tree on a low rise looking down to the shore. Emily removed her shoes and loosened the buttons at her collar and lay back nestling her head on Melville's folded jacket. Whitman unpacked the meal prepared for them early that morning in Downing's kitchen—meat cutlets and bread and fried oysters and raw carrots and ale. In an effort to make the atmosphere amusing, Melville addressed William Johnson.

"William, I expect you've left behind at least one young lady very unhappy over your departure."

"The only lady I've left unhappy down there is my mama, Mr. Melville. I don't go in much for young ladies. I prefer men."

"I see," said Melville, not quite believing what he had just heard.

Emily rose up on her elbows. Whitman blushed. Johnson himself did not seem vexed or embarrassed or up to any mischief.

"You mean romantically?" Emily asked, genuinely astonished.

"Yes, ma'am. Physically speaking, I mean."

"You mean you are not attracted to women?"

"No, Miss Emily. Not in that way. But I like some women very much. The best friends I have ever had have all been women."

"I don't know how things are in South Carolina, William," Melville said, "But up here, I don't recommend you volunteer such information. And if you're asked, better to lie."

"Excellent advice, Mr. Melville," said Whitman. "Seems to me, this young man has troubles enough without having to call down an additional hate mob upon him."

"I am aware," said Johnson, speaking evenly, serenely. "Things in South Carolina, Mr. Melville, could not be worse in this particular respect. I've seen men of my persuasion killed outright in a most gruesome manner even if they were only suspected of such a leaning. I reckon, I just feel comfortable with the three of you."

"That's very brave of you," Emily said.

There followed a predictably awkward silence. Melville fought a powerful urge to stride down to the water's edge, strip, and plunge in. Whitman took a long drink of warm ale, closing his eyes. Then Emily went on.

"But do tell me—only if you wish of course—surely your religion, your bible reading, your own mother even, view such tendencies as sinful."

"They do, Miss Emily, and that is the heaviest cross I bear. But there ain't nothing I can do about it. The soul wants what it wants. It's how God made me, for whatever reason, me and not a small number of other men. I mean, I tried getting on with women that way, if only to attempt to please my mama just like you say, but it never came to anything. It felt as odd and as strange to me as it probably would for you to kiss another girl."

"Now see here, William," said Whitman in a tone of light reprobation.

"Oh, I don't mind," Emily said. "I have to say, I am fascinated. So it must be very hard for you, William."

"Yes, m'am."

"I have heard of such behavior, of course. People whisper about such things in Amherst, but, well I never met . . . or maybe I have. . ."

"It was hard for a long time until I learned my master buttered his bread on the same side as me, and my life began to change after that. I did not have to work as hard on the farm, and it was then I began to plan my escape."

"Your master? Escape?"

Johnson looked at Whitman, realizing his mistake. Whitman took a deep breath and addressed the following looking mostly at Emily.

"Now is as good a time as any, and Lord knows we could use a change of topic. You see, Miss Dickinson, William here was born into slavery and has only recently escaped from a cotton plantation where he lived all his life and I am helping him to safety and to a life of freedom in Boston."

"No . . ."

"Yes, m'am."

"A slave."

"Yes, m'am."

"The underground railway and all of that."

"The very same."

Melville watched her with a smile as she stood up and went over to shake Whitman's hand and then Johnson's. "Let me offer you both a most heartfelt congratulations, for your courage and spirit."

Soon after the entirety of the day's situation had been explained and agreed upon by all, the carriage driver returned bringing a white man with him. Whitman and Melville left Emily and William obscured by the trunk of the elm and walked back to the roadway. The driver presented the man.

"This here is Mr. Emmet Halsey."

"How do you do, Mr. Halsey? I am Walter Whitman and this is my colleague Mr. Herman Melville."

The driver fed his horse some oats from a burlap sack while the three white men conversed.

"It is a thirty-foot sloop based on a beach yawl that was common in England a decade ago. The bowsprit's busted—I ran it into a pier like a damn fool—and though it's still functional thanks to some strong rope, I've found a company in

New London who can replace it and sail it back here but I'm just too busy this time of year to lose a day bringing it over there myself and I want to get it done before autumn."

Melville carried his end of the discussion successfully impressing Halsey with his detailed knowledge of sailing, navigation, and how to best engage the fickle tides of Long Island Sound. Only fifty percent of this experience was practical, the rest he had picked up at sea talking with sailors day after day.

An hour later, Halsey was waving goodbye from a wooden pier at the Greenport marina watching Melville maneuver the sloop out onto Peconic Bay with a nervous first mate scurrying to his instructions. Once Halsey disappeared, they doubled back and landed at the beach near the elm tree and picked up a giggling William and Emily who had to wade into the water up to their thighs.

10

HALF AN HOUR LATER, THE SLOOP CLEARED ORIENT POINT. Plum Island dunes stood off the starboard side as Melville set a north by northeast course across the sound toward Fisher's Island and Groton, Connecticut. The light summer breeze was in their favor and the sails billowed fully. Melville was in high spirits remembering his days on the island of Nuku-heva when taking small sailing skiffs out beyond the reefs was almost a daily occurrence. But here he was on home territory, these were *his* waters and it imbued his feeling of exhilaration with a special poignancy. He was also appreciating the wonders of serendipity, for what time was more propitious than this for him to be out upon these waters with the last section of his manuscript waiting for him back at

Arrowhead? It put him right back into a frame of mind that months spent living inland had diminished.

He held the tiller in the crook of his right arm. Emily and Whitman sat next to each other, their backs leaning against the varnished wood and their feet resting on the bench opposite. William Johnson lay aft upon the deck on his stomach, hugging the repair rope wrapped about the damaged bowsprit, his head peering down with a child's delight, enjoying the wind and the light and how the craft was cutting through the water.

"You two make a handsome couple," Whitman said, all of a sudden after glancing at them. Melville smiled and looked at Emily.

"Yes, we do."

"I am quite certain Mr. and Mrs. Melville make a far handsomer couple still," she replied.

"I would not know," Whitman said, "for I have not had the honor of meeting Mrs. Melville. I can only speak for the here and now. And besides, surely it is possible for one to make a handsome couple with more than just one person."

"I do hope not," she said, far more excited within than she appeared. And she was already in a state of excitement as it was, due to what, for her, was the uncanny and absolutely novel experience of sailing, and on such a vast stretch of sea in such a small boat. To think she had been anxious just the other day when the huge steamer pulled out of the cozy Fall River harbor. But today she was filled with a reckless sense of being alive, the prudish Hawthorne driven into exile, the escaped slave at sea in their hands on his way to freedom, this oafish journalist-poet trying to provoke her, and Melville, inches away at the tiller, body and soul, courting her in flagrant violation of all decency.

"Well, I am afraid it is true," Whitman said. "Don't you agree, Mr. Melville?"

"It appears to be a cultural issue," he said. "I have not read of the opposite being true, but clearly there are many instances of cultures where a man quite naturally takes numerous wives."

"That is abominable!" Emily cried out in a tone akin to joy.

"I am not so sure of that," said Melville. "The number one enemy of the conventional western marriage is the inevitable dulling of the passions through prolonged familiarity. Having more than one spouse relieves some of that, I would think."

"How many wives were you permitted in the South Seas?" Whitman asked, nudging Emily with his elbow. Melville made as if he had not heard and continued with his disquisition.

"Muslims are encouraged to have numerous wives. In ancient Japan the custom was quite common among the upper classes. In Egypt and in Persia there were harems galore. Then, of course, we have our Mormons who practice polygamy, rather joylessly it seems from an outsider's point of view, but without any dire side effects as far as I know."

"Mr. Whitman asked you a question, Armando. How many wives did you have during your pagan idyll in the Marquesas?"

"For your information I did not have even one 'wife' during my time there. Marriage as we know it, does not exist for those people. It is the most extraordinary thing. They have relations with each other, and with foreigners who have the good fortune to land there, based entirely on appetite. I rarely saw or experienced jealousy, for instance."

"If my mother were here she would dive into the sea to drown as a martyr for her faith rather than to have to hear of such a thing."

"And her daughter?" Melville asked.

"Her daughter takes a more scientific view and wonders if such a society as the one you describe so glowingly, so liberated from restrictive Christian morals, might be a society devoid of love."

"An interesting thought," said Whitman.

"I observed a great deal of love during my time there. Both mothers and fathers treated their offspring with inordinate affections, at least until puberty."

"I am referring to romantic love."

"What is romantic love, I wonder?" Whitman asked.

"My question," Emily went on, "is whether your islanders 'fall in love,' or do they just cavort under the coconut trees like upright simians?"

"Did my parents ever fall in love?" Whitman continued. "I am not sure, nor their parents before them. Did your parents fall in love, Miss Dickinson? How about yours, Mr. Melville?"

"I think you do the natives of Nukuheva an injustice, Emily, by likening them to upright simians," Melville said, very gently and looking at her more gently still. She blushed.

"I agree. In a foolish attempt to prove witty it came out flat and untoward. I apologize."

Melville reached across and squeezed her hand and then looked up at the sails. "The western model imagines a couple taking a fancy to each other, then, assuming their parents and their social circle approves, attempting a process through which each sees the other as a unique and ideal solution to their loneliness and needs. A commitment is made, a marriage takes place, an initial period of romantic reverie occurs, or doesn't, property is acquired, children are born, routines are established. The primary romantic spark, if it was ever truly there, cedes to a lower, steadier flame, to a dynamic of prolonged mutual dependence. They become a team, parents, citizens in their community. Can we agree on this?"

"Yes," said Emily.

"At least for argument's sake, yes," said Whitman.

"As to Mr. Whitman's question whether, within that template, our respective parents had that initial period of romantic enchantment poets and troubadours have been going on about since the time of Arthur and Gwenevere—speaking for my own parents I am fairly certain they did."

"Then they were fortunate indeed," Whitman said. "I am hard pressed to imagine my parents enjoying anything remotely akin to romantic grace."

"I must say, neither can I," Emily said.

William Johnson, holding onto what he could, made his way back and joined them. Whitman put his feet down and Johnson sat facing him.

"What do you make of sea travel, Mr. Johnson?" Melville asked.

"That it is both an unnatural thing for a man to do, and that it is a miracle."

"I quite agree with you William," Emily said.

"Laying down up there at the front of the boat I felt all my troubles lift. They were carried off by the wind."

"There you have one of every sailor's main motivations for setting out upon the main," Melville said.

"Tell us, William," Emily said, "did you know your father, or know if your mother and father had fallen in love with each other?"

"My father was chosen by the plantation foreman and my mother was held down until the man was done with her while the master and his friends stood around and watched, and that happened repeatedly until she was some months on with child and they let her be—picking out some other couple for their sinful diversion."

The three listeners remained silent.

"The master and his friends liked to watch that and to watch the whippings late after their evening meal when the women folk retired and the whiskey was flowing and on more than one occasion, I have been told there were women present as well. I was never formally introduced to my father. He was father to a number of us. He was a proud and sullen man who paid no attention to his offspring. And no, neither my father nor my mother had any opportunity to enjoy the luxury of courting."

Emily leaned forward and took Johnson's hand in hers. Whitman looked up toward the jib. Melville finally spoke. "That is a terrible thing, William. A terrible thing for which there can be no forgiveness. We can only hope that, from now on, you will have a much better future than your kin since they were brought in chains to this odd land of ours."

"The Old Testament talks about an eye for an eye," Johnson said. "And the New Testament talks of turning the other cheek."

"Which testament do you favor?"

"I love Jesus, but I am more at home with Genesis."

Shortly after this conversation, both Whitman and Johnson returned to the prow of the sloop to talk, their hair and clothing blowing in the brisk breeze. Emily took advantage of the vacant space and lay down for a nap as Melville kept the sloop on course. He looked at her now and then, restraining himself from the urge to place a hand upon her shoulder or to feel her cheek with the backs of his fingers or to smell her hair.

An hour later, Emily awakened nestled on the cockpit bench in the shade of flapping sails. She looked up past the tip of the mast and took in the bluest sky she had ever seen. A late afternoon summer tenderness had taken possession of the light and aether. The boat was still and water lapped against the hull and she felt a powerful urge to pee and realized it was this pelvic prompting that had roused her from a slumber she could barely recall giving in to. Then, sitting up she saw something she had never seen before.

The boat was anchored in shallow, clear water, just some two yards from a sandbar that extended from an empty stretch of beach along the leeward shore of an island that seemed uninhabited. Further in beach grass and dusty miller grew in the dunes and further in still thickets and green shrubbery were alive with birds and wild flowers. But what most drew her attention were the naked figures of Whitman and William Johnson laying next to each other on the sand by the water's edge holding each other.

She lay down again immediately, her heart racing as if it had been she herself caught in *flagrante delicto*. Where the deuce was Melville, she asked herself partly frightened at the thought that in a fit of disgust he may have abandoned her there with the two sodomites. So, Whitman too was one of them! The special respect she had held him in for the altruism he was demonstrating by risking his skin to contribute to the cause of human freedom, exemplifying an active Christian will to do good that she had held Melville somewhat in fault for lacking—fell like the proverbial house of cards, swept away by a sordid wind of depravity and self-interest.

But upon further reflection, she had to admit that there was nothing in the posture of the two men she saw tossed together upon the beach that indicated coercion or skullduggery. They had both of them appeared equally enthralled by the sensations they were imparting to each other.

Slowly she raised her head again, fascinated by this Decameron tableau, and then she looked the other way, scouring the view for Melville. Further along the strand of shore in this more easterly direction she did see something that resembled his clothing left in a heap. She looked out off the stern and saw him swimming, saw him swimming like a creature born to it, employing massive lazy strokes with his arms and breathing from side to side, heading further out to sea. Trusting in providence that he would not return at once and that the two individuals nearer by condemning themselves to a fiery afterlife would continue to do so for at least another minute, she tugged off her petticoats, raised the skirt of her dress and, taking hold of a line cleat, leaned her naked bottom over the side and emptied her bladder. It was at just this moment when Melville stopped swimming, ceasing his crawl, and began to tread water. As a matter of course, he turned to see how much distance had put between himself and the sloop. It was most definitely Emily's naked derriere he saw, aimed his way with such precision he at first considered the absurd proposition she was doing it to taunt him. Then, and not without a certain measure of compassion, he realized what she was doing. He considered calling out to her but had not the heart, and worried she might find it terminally rude. Before initiating the swim back, he allowed himself the luxury of a voyeur's delight wondering where the other two had disappeared to. He was too far away to make out her anatomy with anything resembling clinical detail but close enough to appreciate, and react to—cold water and all—the delicious gamine curves revealed thanks to her predicament. What a wondrous thing nature could be and what a glorious marvel was the female form. All he could really make out was her lower back, smooth and slight and white and then the telltale curves at either side that so gracefully budded and became the sweetly rounded cheeks of her naked arse.

And then it was over. With a strength he would not have expected her capable of, she pulled herself back into the cockpit of the sloop in one fluid motion. Swimming back to shore he contemplated to what extent his state of enchantment derived from the feelings he had for her and what part from the novelty she represented. He had to admit there had been a time when viewing the posterior of his own Elizabeth would have provoked him into a similar state and it grieved him to recognize that was no longer the case. Why? What was it about familiarity that sated one's interest? It also altered behavior. He had been far more attentive to Elizabeth's wants and needs at the beginning, just as she had been far more flirtatious with him. Now their sense of "coupledom" had been worn down through exposure, through children and the constant presence of other family members, his own mother for example, sleeping in the bedroom immediately adjacent to theirs. Come to think of it, he thought to himself, he had never spent time with Elizabeth similar to the time he had been passing these past few days with Emily.

When Emily peeked back toward the fornicators, they had finished their dalliance and were dressing, sitting up on the damp sand. Turning the other way she caught a glimpse of Melville emerging from the sea naked as Adam before The Fall, striding up to where his clothes lay and standing there a few moments allowing the gentle sun to partially dry his gleaming skin. He presented a handsome, primitive vision of raw masculinity she had also never seen before and it moved her. Up until that afternoon, men had been creatures one always saw clothed, often excessively so, and then today without warning she found herself surrounded by all manner of virile nudity. She could not help but feel there was something shameful in it. This too was true.

When they sailed into New London two hours later it was twilight and all four of them were quiet, each with their own set of agitated cogitations. Melville found the pier Emmet Halsey had described, and soon had the sloop securely moored. He knocked on the ship carpenter's dockside workshop door just minutes before it was to close for the evening and the four travelers left the area on foot together with their mission accomplished.

Whitman had a name for an inn, The Cardinal's Deck, where William Johnson could be put up safely for the night, and just as it grew dark they found it. The front door, painted red, was flanked by two lilac shrubs in full bloom and the smell was intoxicating flooding both Emily and Melville with childhood memories. The owner was a stocky and broadminded Frenchman called René Miron, descended from early trappers and whose grandfather, like Melville's, had fought the British during the American Revolution. This and the fact that Melville's late father had done most of his business in Paris, won the man over immediately, and their appetites, accentuated by the day's excitements and the paltry midday fare, were soon being attended to by *une grande bouffe* prepared with great gaulic gumption.

Dominating one of the dining room's walls was a portrait of Cardinal Richelieu.

"How many of you have read *The Three Musketeers*?" asked their host in a French accent Melville was fairly certain the man had no cause for. It seemed all of them had read it with the understandable exception of William Johnson.

"Just as I thought. And how many of you realize the author was a complete idiot?!" He gave this last word a distinctly French pronunciation delivered in unison with a thick slug of cork that popped from a deep green bottle of champagne and ricocheted off the low ceiling. He proceeded to fill their glasses. "Dumas presents the Cardinal as a villain, a calculating knave bejeweled with garish rings and bedecked in foppish liturgical clothing just to give his child's tale a touch of simplistic adventure." Here he paused for effect. "Richelieu was responsible for *La France* as we know it, was the first Prime Minister. The man was responsible for allowing Samuel de Champlain to establish a vibrant French colony in the heart of North America."

Melville raised his glass, pointing it toward the painting. "To the Cardinal." They all followed suit. "And to France," he continued.

"And to *liberté, egalité, fraternité*," said Miron raising his glass yet again and gesturing toward William Johnson.

Everyone was feeling quite pleased with themselves at this point. Johnson pushed his chair back and stood.

"I too would like to speak a toast," he said. "I ain't never seen a black man do so and I reckon now's a good a time as any."

"Here-here!" said Whitman with a nervous enthusiasm Emily took note of.

"I don't know what this nice man just said, speaking in a language I do not understand. But I can tell by how he said it that he meant well by me. Some of you have made light of my Bible learning, but all of you have been most respectful of me, and of where I come from, and all of you have been so helpful in getting me to where I am going. I know that I myself am a sinful man. . ." and here tears came into his eyes and his mouth began to quiver and the rest of them went very still and Emily leaned forward especially enrapt. "I am a sinful man who cannot help himself and who wonders sometimes why the Lord does these things to his children. The only answer that occurs to me is that we are in need of daily reminders, reminders of who we really are and of why we are here on this Earth and of how easy the Lord's tests of our goodness and moral worthiness really are compared to the infinite dimensions of the afterlife."

Emily and Whitman correctly assumed he was repenting for what had happened earlier that day on the beach. Melville and the Frenchman, hungry and eager to get on with the meal, made no conjectures of any kind.

"For what is the span of a man's life compared with eternity? As my mama once described it—pretend she said—that a dove flies by the highest mountain once every ten years and with its wing grazes its peak or a boulder, knocking off a piece of it no bigger than a grain of sand. By the time the entire mountain has eroded by virtue of this process, the entire mountain reduced to sand upon a plain—not one second of eternity would have elapsed."

His eyes were sparkling now with fervor from this remembered metaphor of maternal origin while the glasses of champagne were beginning to weigh upon the raised wrists of his captive audience—Melville intuiting a fine

career ahead for Johnson as a preacher—when mercy intervened—Johnson bowing his handsome head and saying,
"Amen."

All four of them drained their glasses. What impressed
Emily was the contrast between Johnson's tone of remorse
for his actions and Whitman's seeming indifference, an
impression that only served to confirm her often-felt belief
that she still had much to learn about human behavior.

"William," she said, "I fervently hope you do not think I
ever made light of your religious vocation."

"No, ma'am. You know the scriptures forwards and back-
wards."

"He was referring to me," Melville said with a grin. "Am
I right, Mr. Johnson?"

The freed slave just smiled and looked down.

"You must pray for me, William," Melville added, "Just,
and at the request of my dear mother, as the ministers do in
Pittsfield, Massachusetts."

"I pray for all of you."

Monsieur Miron had had his fill of Christian banter and
somewhat blamed himself for perhaps starting it all with his
spirited defense of *Le Eminence Rouge*. Reaching for a bottle of
Mercurey Premier Cru and summoning in the meat with a nod
of his head, he turned to his favored guest. "Have you been to
Montreal, Mr. Melville?"

After the dinner of roasted lamb and new corn and apple
crumble, René Miron belching unabashedly excused himself
to attend to other guests. Melville and Emily decided to take
a postprandial stroll, and Whitman, yawning in a somewhat
theatrical fashion, pleaded exhaustion and announced he was
going to sleep. William Johnson followed suit. And thus it
was the two couples said goodbye to each other in the inn's

lobby at the foot of the stairs promising to write and to see each other again. Melville made a special point of telling Johnson that he should not hesitate to contact him were he to ever find himself in trouble.

"I shall be forever grateful, Mr. Melville. May God bless you and protect you and your family and may you do your best to learn from Miss Emily's wisdom."

"That I shall, William."

Emily shook his hand with tears in her eyes. Whitman took some folded pages of yellowed newspaper from his pocket, torn a month earlier from the *New York Daily Tribune* and handed them to Melville.

"Here is a copy of a recent poem, Mr. Melville. I would be very much obliged if you might take the time to read it."

Melville looked at the title "Resurgemus." "I assure you I will."

"And I will send you and Mr. Hawthorne copies of the interview once I get that published as well."

"We both look forward to it."

Outside it was a damp July night. Dew adorned the grass. Lightning bugs were hovering and twinkling low over the ground and the smell of salt water permeated the air. The moon, fuller now than when last seen in New York, provided just the right amount of light needed to make their way along the dockside section of Pequot Avenue and then along the country lane it turned into. Upon seeing the street sign, Melville was taken aback, for he had bastardized the same word taken from what had been the name of the local Indian tribe to name his ship in *Moby-Dick*! He seized upon it as an initial theme of conversation until the increasing darkness and distance from the inn imposed a rich silence upon them.

Although framed differently in each of them, the thought uppermost in both their minds, one that wound its way through their blood, creating a collective state of nervous tension, was the knowledge they were alone—alone together for what might be the only time in their lives. Austin and Hawthorne were many miles away. The elder Dickinsons as well. And now, even Whitman and William Johnson had retired for the night. They were alone and walking together in the summer night where no one knew them or could see them. Rather than give voice to this obvious and startling fact—and for the moment struggling to avoid it altogether—Emily resorted to a declaration she had earlier decided not to share with anyone.

"I witnessed the most extraordinary thing today when you were off swimming."

"It has been an extraordinary day."

"I'm not certain how to put this with any delicacy . . . I saw Mr. Whitman and Mr. Johnson engaged in—speaking most kindly and metaphorically—amorous activity."

"No."

"Yes."

"What kind of amorous activity?"

She covered her mouth with one of her hands. He began to laugh.

"Shhh. You mustn't make light of it."

"Why not?"

"I am still recovering from it."

"Nonsense," he said, taking advantage of the moment to touch her gently on her back and savoring the sensation, "you are a dramatist of the highest order, Emily. What were they doing?"

"Touching each other."

"Where?"

"You know perfectly well where."

"No!"

"Yes. The two of them naked as your beloved savages."

"Where were they?"

"Down at the very end of that empty beach, while you were swimming and when I was supposedly sound asleep."

"I looked back at one point and could not see them. I suppose the sloop was in the way."

"You looked back?"

"Yes," he said smiling to himself. "I did."

"Oh, dear."

"Why?" He managed to inflect the question with believable innocence.

"Nothing."

"Poor Emily."

"I have never been so astonished in all my life. And I had never expected Mr. Whitman to be so inclined. So at first I suspected the very worst."

"Being . . ."

"That Mr. Whitman's interest in William's 'freedom' was so that he might exploit the poor man like the fellow's 'master' had down South."

"But Mr. Johnson had already confessed to us all his . . . his predilection—one he seems quite resigned to despite his somewhat melodramatic religious aims."

"Yes. I did come to realize that. I suppose I am hopelessly naïve."

He could not recall feeling happier than he did at that moment. Walking with her like this as if it were the most natural thing in the world, engaging her mind and her wit, her particular sensibility, here on this exemplary geographic extension of their home environs. "To the extent you might be considered naïve it becomes you most graciously. On the other hand, you are not all that naïve. My very first impression of you was of someone very quick, very alert, whose mind never ceased observing."

"I imagine you know that you can be dangerously charming sometimes."

"It is not a pose. I am simply reporting my genuine impressions."

"That day we first saw each other, it feels like weeks ago, does it not?"

"Months."

"And yet only a few days have transpired. Time is a great mystery."

"It may be *the* great mystery."

"I feel quite bad about Mr. Hawthorne. The two of you were in such good spirits together that day."

"And so shall we be again."

"I am gladdened to hear it. Did you suspect Mr. Whitman?"

"Of being a sodomite?"

"Yes."

"No. I mean I hadn't thought about it one way or the other. Some of them are easy to identify, of course, but many others can appear to be quite normal."

"The way they are *is* normal for them."

"Now there's a point not often made. Aboard ship, at sea for months and months at a time, one sees all manner of behavior."

"I hadn't thought of that. More naïveté!"

"I suppose it is a bit like what I hear goes on in prisons."

"How appalling."

"Of course one is sent to prison. No one goes voluntarily, whereas almost everyone who goes to sea does so of his own accord, which begs the question—do they do so because a number of them are already of the sodomite persuasion, knowing they will encounter others of their ilk, living in close quarters with hardly any privacy at all, or do the conditions themselves cause certain men to behave in such a manner, men who revert to being with women and wives once they are back in port? I expect it is a mixture."

"You were at sea a very long time, no?"

"Yes. But I never resorted to such a thing."

"You had your native women . . ."

"Neither did half of the crew at the very least and none of the officers that I was aware of. There was a common activity among those seamen I was referring to known as taking 'chaw for chaw,' resembling scenes one sometimes must suffer at the monkey house in a zoo."

"This is what they were doing."

"Who?"

"Who do you think?"

"Ah! Poor Emily. I expect you felt a long way from Amherst."

"I did."

"And how do you feel now?"

"Closer. And I wish you would desist from referring to me as 'poor' Emily."

"I shall never do so again—and tomorrow I shall deliver you back to the family homestead."

She did not say anything to this and they walked along for half a minute in silence. He regretted the conversation so rid-

dled with sexual content of a nature virtually designed to put
one off physical contact of any description for a good while.
But she was not nearly as perturbed about it as he imagined.
In some odd and unexpected way it even stimulated her. She
was more aware that she had brought the topic up in the first
place so as to have something to say at all, and the topic in
question, this unbeknownst to her, was chosen as a substitute
for her own sexual stirrings that, unnamed, had never been
more present than they were that evening.

"Where were we today?" she asked him. "Where was that
beach?"

He was relieved to have a new path of conversation. "It
was the western end of Fisher's Island, some seven miles
south of here. It was Whitman, of course, who suggested we
stop for a rest. You were already asleep."

"It was very beautiful. It felt like some place very far
away, for me at least, or like a place preserved in a state akin
to what it must have been like before any European blood
arrived here."

"I had the very same thought. The same feeling."

"I felt absurdly overdressed and resented the freedom
you men had to so affix yourselves with Nature there, some
of you in different ways of course."

"You could have joined me in my swim."

"I do not know how, nor did you think to awaken me to
ask."

"I would love to teach you how to swim."

"You know that will never happen."

"So much could happen if we would just allow it."

"Who is the naïve one now? For a man your age who has
been through so much and who is such a keen observer of
society, these statements you make surprise me."

"Have you considered the possibility that precisely due to my age and experience and power of observation that what I am suggesting may not be that outlandish?"

"No. And what are you suggesting, really? That, based on a three day flirtation you are prepared to leave your child and your pregnant wife and to ask for my hand in the Dickinson household? Are you completely mad?"

"Is that what this is to you? A flirtation?"

"How else could I define it?"

He stopped, and took hold of her, and turned her to him, and kissed her. In an instant they realized, in a manner that made a mockery of words and intellectual reasoning, that this is what they had both been wanting, and fiercely, since their predawn embrace upon the deck of the steamer. Their timidity and practiced decorum vanished as their hearts raced and as their tongues intertwined. Supporting her back with one arm he lifted her from the ground with the other and brought the two of them down upon the wet grass where they continued to kiss ferociously. He placed a hand against her breast and through the layers of linen and cotton felt the nipple harden as he himself felt a craven need to burst into her. She could feel him pushing upon her as he lay on top of her and she did not care. The thin sliver of sense that remained in her mind gone feverish told her that this, in all likelihood, would be a moment like no other that she would reenact until the day she died. It was only when his hand cupped her garments between her legs and when he began to lift the hem of her dress that her father's daughter regained possession of her.

"Don't," she said, pulling her mouth away from him. "Please."

He stopped at once—looked at her—came to his own senses and rolled off of her onto his back beside her. They lay like that in silence until he finally spoke.

"I'm sorry."

She felt for his hand, found and squeezed it, and kept it in hers.

"I believe I am much sorrier than you," she said.

He rose and helped her to her feet. The combined and contradictory emotions of elation and frustration were so present in the night air between them that they both chose to remain silent, heading back, hand in hand, in the direction of the inn. He saw her to her room, bid her goodnight kissing her hand, and retired to his quarters overlooking the harbor convinced his intimacies with Emily Dickinson had come to an end. He went to sleep preparing himself for the following day's return to Arrowhead.

But a summer squall blew in that night and Emily awakened in her bed entranced by the thunder and lightning about her and by the noise of the heavy rain beating down upon the wooden shingles of the roof above her. The effects of the champagne and the burgundy had worn off and she felt cozy and safe and relieved to be less than a day's journey from Amherst. She wondered how Austin had fared and whether he would be there to meet her tomorrow evening at the appointed spot so that they could successfully complete their mad ruse returning to the house together. She wondered how her mother and Lavinia were, and her father still in Washington. What had become of the Spanish Duchess? Fiona? Might William Johnson be in Whitman's room tonight hearing the rain, and what would become of him set on his own at last in Boston? She perused these thoughts in a leisurely but thorough fashion because she already knew what she was going to do and felt the need to "clean the slate" first.

A minute later in her nightgown and barefeet she was opening the unlocked door to Melville's room. He stirred as she got into his bed. They looked at each other, lying on their sides facing each other in the dark, and then kissed.

"I could not bear to spend this last night apart from you."

He embraced her and squeezed her tight. "Bless you," he said.

"And I know I can trust you," she said.

"That you can."

And so they lay there like that, like lovers, in the dark near a large window opened a crack so that the rain smell and the thunder noise were with them. Eventually their hands wandered, as hands are wont to do in such moments of grace, and their lips found each other again and though Emily remained a virgin, she experienced an orgasm that caused her to cry out in wonder. And shortly afterward, holding him the way she had seen William Johnson and Whitman holding each other earlier that day, she heard her lover's own muffled groan and felt warm sticky alkaline drops of his semen covering her hands and bodice. They fell asleep together before the rain ceased, smiling and sated and filled with a conspirator's contentment.

She left him snoring around five and met William Johnson in the corridor as he emerged from Whitman's door. A simultaneous rush of embarrassment and affection coursed through them and they merely nodded to each other before retiring toward their own rooms. Then William Johnson stopped, and turned and walked back to her just as she was about to close her door.

"We are all God's children," he said in a whisper.

"Amen," she answered in kind.

"Have mercy on me Oh God in your great kindness: in the fullness of your mercy blot out my offenses," he said.

She smiled and replied, "Wash away all my guilt: and cleanse me from my sin."

"For I acknowledge my faults: and my sin is always before me."

"Against you only have I sinned," she said.

"Evil have I been from my birth: sinner I am from the time of my conception."

She kissed him on the cheek before closing her door definitively. "But you desire truth in our inward being," she said, "therefore teach me wisdom in my secret heart."

11

THE EARTH CONTINUED ITS JOURNEY ABOUT THE SUN spinning about its own axis, atilt in such a manner that an hour later dawn appeared along the coast of Newfoundland and New England. The village of New London began to stir. Many of the elderly were already up and dressed. Kettles were on the boil as eggs were retrieved from backyard hencoops. Infants cried out for succor and fishing boats prepared to cast off for the day. Overfed summer residents and guests in bed at the local inns still fluttered their eyes beneath closed lids enrapt in dreams. Back on the western tip of Fisher's Island, bluefish were running, frothing the gray-blue surface of the water, all trace of human prints having disappeared overnight. Horseshoe crabs crawled upon the damp sand.

As the day broke and they awakened, both Melville and Emily fought any obligation to rise from their respective beds. They knew full well that once the process began, this final day of traveling would take on its own hue and clamor and get about its work of obliterating the treasured sense of calm and intimacy still there under the covers. They listened to the birds outside, smelling tides and honeysuckle.

Although she had not given herself to him completely, she certainly had given enough to be disqualified from continuing to maintain her moral high ground, protesting his advances, or admonishing him with references to his wife and family. He, in turn, was reluctant to push any harder. In the humid glaze of that July morning, after devouring an excessively rich French breakfast, he was painfully aware of the fact that each of them would be spending that night away from the other, their journey over and done.

Thus it was that during the warm and arduous trip north, through Norwich and Colchester and Hartford, entering Massachusetts at Longmeadow and then pushing up into Springfield and Holyoke before entering North Hadley in the early evening—they said very little. Occasionally they would hold hands and touch each other briefly when pointing out one thing or another. What conversation they did have was devoted mostly to Shakespeare and to *Jane Eyre*, which Emily had read the year before, and both of them took delight in reviewing the days they had spent together since setting out for Boston. The smallest details acquired inordinate significance. There was little discussion devoted to the future, except for when he spoke about the upcoming visit to the Berkshires planned with the Duyckincks, the Hawthornes, and the Morewoods. What Emily most wanted to hear about were his thoughts and worries about *Moby-Dick*.

"What is it about the final day of a trip that makes it feel so elusive?" he asked her all of a sudden. "No matter how long that day might be, and this has been a long one indeed, one still discounts it in a way."

"I discount nothing. You are living in the future today, and I in the recent past."

"I envy you that. I truly wish we were starting out all over again."

As agreed, the siblings met each other at a tavern in North Hadley, a small hamlet close to and southwest from Amherst. Melville found Austin distant, haggard, and—how to put it?—chastened. Clearly something had happened to his grand plan. And Austin had to pretend surprise at not seeing Hawthorne along with them, an emotion facilitated considerably due to the actual surprise it gave him to see them without Mr. Whitman either.

"Nathaniel jumped ahead of us, back on the steamer. I'm surprised you did not see him on board. We parted company with Mr. Whitman early this morning before he went on to Boston."

"In any event, here you are and my sister is safe and sound."

"That I am," she said, taking his arm.

Melville had meant to say goodbye separately to Emily before this family rendezvous took place but the right occasion had never presented itself and now the moment of their final farewell was suddenly and unglamorously before them.

They shook hands and looked into each other's eyes for the briefest moment. Folded between her delicate fingers was a small sheet of paper she passed on to him. Then they were gone. He watched them leave and waved to them once and then found himself alone. He did not unfold the piece of paper until over an hour later when he checked into the inn where he and Hawthorne had stayed and left their horses a week earlier. In the narrow, dark stables at the back of the building, surrounded by hay dust and harnesses and saddles and the smell of manure, kissing his horse on its strong neck and patting it down—for here was another creature he was connected to—he read what she had written . . .

Come slowly, Eden!
Lips unused to thee,
Bashful, sip thy jasmines,
As the fainting bee,

Reaching late his flower,
Round her chamber hums,
Counts his nectars—enters,
And is lost in balms!

The narrowness of his bed at the austere lodging house that evening called forth two realizations: Never had the prospect of returning to the comforts of his life at Arrowhead been more appealing, and that the frenzied, dark, shame-laced couplings so common in his part of the world, so hidden, so rushed, so awkward as a rule, stood in stark contrast to what sex had been like during his stay on the Marquesas Islands. There, time was taken, smiles abounded, relaxing oils were applied, there was an easy joyfulness to it he sorely missed that night. What had Christianity wrought upon his northern brethren? Or perhaps it was simply a question of

climate—but he doubted it—for the Puritans did not let
their hair down or open their bodices any easier with the
arrival of summer. Last night's interaction had held fast to
that course. His was a culture of worry and prohibition.

He lay there for a spell, weaving dreams . . . Emily with
him on Nukuheva, her hair flowing, a gardenia behind an ear,
wearing nothing but a sarong, her gentle breasts exposed,
strolling with him along the beach, continuing their conversation about Shakespeare, about whom her erudition had
bowled him over, while hearing the whispering surf and the
gentle rhythms of swaying palm fronds, and then the two
of them indulging each other, liberated from their world of
starch and pale skin. But once he ejaculated into the void and
returned reluctantly to the present, afflicted with an empty
sensation he knew too well, he delved further into the Puritan ethos. He remembered Emily's question from the other
day as to whether his free-spirited noble savages were capable of falling in love. He thought it a defensive aspersion at
the time, tinged with a degree of racism and condescension.
But he had to admit, confined within the dark and humid
New England night that there was some substance to her
inquiry. If love is free and too easily available then what is its
value, and is it in fact love? He came to recognize that when
he told her his tales of what his life as a mutineer on the
islands had been like, episodes he had managed to capital-
ize on through his first two books, he allowed himself a significant degree of poetic license and that by relating them so
often and with such conviction he had reached a point, now
some years ago, where he actually believed the more fanciful
bits as if they had actually occurred. Perhaps many memories were like that, rudimentary reportages dressed up and
expanded upon by the imagination, like the very fictions he

wrote so laboriously. He recalled many an evening after a hard day's work on *Moby-Dick* when he drifted off into sleep convinced he had actually taken part in Ahab's manic hunt. And, of course, the adornments inevitably took their place in order to improve upon the rudimentary, to make one-self more sympathetic, more pronounced, more attractive, to sculpt people and events into more pleasing or dramatic shapes, to illume them with a more favorable or despicable light.

There he lay in the dark, the cool night air entering through the window. Emily and her brother were once again captives in their impressive house on the other side of town. Was she, too, in her bed thinking of him or might she be already erasing their days together relieved to be home and eager to reestablish her reliable domestic routines? He made an effort to demythologize his personal narrative, to sepa-rate reliable wheat from his own invented chaff, and he was forced thus to recall that his actual liaisons with the native woman he called Fayaway derived their piquancy more from the allure of her being so thoroughly "the other" than because of her personal charm. Not speaking the other's lan-guage allowed for a freedom from inhibition and offered all manner of opportunity for imbuing the other with depths and sensibilities that in all likelihood were not there. To the extent there had been any complicity at all between them, it was of the sort small children form playing primitive games articulated with primitive vocabularies. When he told his exotic sea tales, he omitted the mosquito bites, the rashes, the foul smells, the filthy feet, and oily hair. So, perhaps his own civilization's mores were not entirely reprehensible. The complicity he experienced dialoging with Hawthorne and the Duyckinck brothers, with Elizabeth—the extraordinary complicity he felt in Emily's company, all of it using the currency of precise language—was head and shoulders above the sign language and awkward smiles he had employed day after day in the Marquesas.

And had the sex really been all that sensual? Perhaps from a strictly plumbing point of view it had—but there had been no lust, no compelling desire even close to the kind they had both felt last night in New London. He should like to tell her that, to relieve her of the misconception he had glibly allowed her to entertain about his rakish past in the South Pacific and in the brothels of Peru. All of that, upon closer inspection, now seemed much more awkward and labored than the New England rituals of courtship, like some prolonged adolescent phase of prurient experimentation engaged in not from genuine desire or excess affection, but rather as fodder to store for future braggadocio—which—he was now compelled to admit as well—had been the overwhelming impetus for his early literary works. Prolonged nudity upon the islands was a great lust leveler, whereas the unexpected grace of seeing Emily's naked bottom the other day ran its electrical current through him from stem to stern. Feeling her smooth, delicious wetness with his gently probing fingers under the flimsy skirt of her nightgown, licking her bare nipples in the dark of his room—all of that—for however limited and cloistered by Puritan injunction had set fire to his heart.

12

"That day, 1 August, Melville celebrated his thirty-second birthday by making an unannounced visit to Hawthorne, who just then was keeping Bachelor's Hall with five-year-old Julian, Sophia having left with Una to display the baby to the Peabody and Hawthorne families. Hawthorne made this account in his journal:

> Returning to the Post office got Mr. Tappan's mail and my own and proceeded homeward, but clambered over the fence and sat down in Love Grove to read the papers. While thus engaged, a cavalier on horseback came along the road, and saluted me in Spanish; to which I replied by touching my hat, and went on with the newspaper. But the cavalier renewing his salutation, I regarded

him more attentively, and saw that it was Herman Melville! So, hereupon, Julian and I hastened to the road, where ensued a greeting, and we all went homeward together, talking as we went. Soon, Mr. Melville alighted, and put Julian into the saddle; and the little man was highly pleased, and sat on the horse with the freedom and fearlessness of an old equestrian, and had a ride of at least a mile homeward."

HERMAN MELVILLE—A BIOGRAPHY, VOLUME 1, 1819–1851—
BY HERSHEL PARKER

Growing up is not for the faint of heart, and given that, for so many, being faint of heart forms an integral part of being human, growing up is difficult. The various ways of steeling the heart, the complicated mixtures of how we do it to ourselves and of how it is done to us, determine what kind of adults we become. But Julian Hawthorne was only five that day, his own ration of steeling hovering about in a still-distant future. He went to sleep a happy little boy that evening, secure in his father's affection, kindly attended to by Miss Potter, kissed goodnight by his father's energetic and extravagant friend.

At his request, the door to his bedroom was left slightly ajar. The sounds of the adult male voices talking and laughing in the salon completed the boy's notion of felicity. Miss Potter set some food out for the two gentlemen and bid them adieu. As they clinked their glasses of wine, Melville made no mention of his birthday.

"How was your journey back?" he asked, looking out upon the gently sloping lawn.

"Long, hot, humid, and dull and only relieved to some small extent by my trusty volume of Livy's *History of Rome*. But the question surely is not—how was my journey back but rather, how was yours!"

"Where to begin?"

"Ah, and before you do—I'd like to apologize—somewhat—for my unctuous attitude of disapproval. I think I was frustrated for reasons of my own, and a tad jealous, and irritated by having our own fine time taken over by the young Dickinsons I, myself, brought into the mix."

"I, too, am sorry, Nathaniel, and we must make it up to each other. Even Emily felt bad about it."

"All is forgiven, all the way round. And now that you have deigned to mention her name . . . out with it man! Are you still bewitched? Is the firmament about to break asunder beneath the foundations of Arrowhead?"

Melville then related the events of his own return trip from Manhattan, beginning with the dinner party at the Morewoods that Hawthorne had excused himself from, and ending with his taking leave of Emily and Austin at the tavern in Hadley now just a week ago. He omitted no detail except for what had transpired between he and Emily along the path and then in his room at The Cardinal's Deck in New London.

"Don't you feel better, sleep easier, converse with Lizzie more lightheartedly for having comported yourself throughout like a gentleman with Miss Dickinson?"

"I had not given it much thought."

"I am sure that you do. And imagine the relief Emily feels, rejoined with her parents who reacted to our ill-conceived invitation with such understandable displeasure."

"Yes, I have thought about that."

"Imagine if you had seduced her, laid siege to her frag-ile ramparts with all that Melvillian charm, for a moment or two of pleasure, even for a short-lived romantic idyll? Betraying the trust of your beloved wife like some common cad . . ."

"May I say something?"

"By all means."

"Just a moment ago, when you seemed impatient for me to spill the goods, it sounded like you were perhaps prepared to hear almost anything. It even seemed as if you were rel-ishing the possibility of hearing news of the most 'caddish' behavior possible."

"I am only a man, Herman. I confess it." He laughed. "Weak as any of us and as prone to the paltry thrills of gossip as the next. But upon hearing what actually happened, I am bursting with relief. I feel ashamed for having doubted you."

Melville smiled with not a whit of condescension or irony, very glad to be rejoined with his more conservative friend. Despite their difference in age and personal quirks, he knew full well they were both examples, even allowing for the unusual fact that they were writers, of what proper society asked for in terms of marriage and manners. They were both espoused to fine women, both had handsome children, both did all they could to provide for their fam-ily's wellbeing, both had servants and esteemed in-laws, and both, he knew but could not say, felt hemmed in and gener-ally emasculated by it all. He also realized neither Elizabeth nor Sophia were to blame. They, too, were human and in possession of a full compliment of instincts and desires.

While Hawthorne excused himself to go pee upon the lawn, Melville, and not for the first time, imagined how his life might be were he to announce his new affections to Lizzie and his family, to live apart from them and to attempt a new life with Emily. The initial surge of romantic emotion that overcame him accompanied an additional sensation of heart-swell particular to the self-destructive impulses common to the rebellious personality—carefully hued scenes flowed through his brain of he and Emily sharing a bed, swimming in Melville lake, having a child, reading together, walking the streets of Paris—but then he felt the tug of gravity pulling him down to reality's stony terrain. And there he was forced to recognize that it would be his financial ruin if such a thing were ever to happen, his dependence on the generosity that emanated from Judge Shaw's deep pockets, how all of that would affect any life he and Emily might have a chance at sharing. The romantic moments would fall by the wayside rolled over by an incessant clamor from bill collectors and the daily drudge that life can become defined by. They would grow thin and destitute and end up eking out a life of need and misery eventually coming to resent each other for having brought such disgrace upon lives that theretofore had been blessed with stability and well-stocked larders.

Hawthorne returned and took notice of the somber expression upon his neighbor's visage.

"So, there I was, raining a steady stream of uric acid down upon ants and beetles and an unfortunate worm perhaps. Me standing there by the stately oak at peace with my world, breathing in the sweet night air, my son asleep and safe in the house behind me, my good friend here awaiting me, all the while wreaking suffering and death on those small creatures hidden amongst the blades of grass."

"As my Ahab says, *the truth shall drive thee mad*, Nathaniel."

"What are we to make of it? It's as if a shower of meteors were to suddenly choose this spot on which to fall, sending you and I and dear Julian to Kingdom Come."

Melville slowly lit a cigar before answering.

"It can get far darker still . . . are you sure there *is* a Kingdom Come?"

"Of course, I am not. But there devil well better be!"

"I expect luck has more to do with life and existence than either of us would feel comfortable admitting. Where many see the will or the hand of God there may be little more than a pair of rickety dice rolling *sans* rhyme or reason."

They sat in silence, smoking, for a good while.

"Are you really a Christian, Herman?"

"Are you?"

"I examine my conscience about this often, especially as I am growing older, and I have to say, even after taking into account all of my many doubts, complaints, and exasperations, that yes, I am. The universe is just too bleak and black without it."

"I honestly do not know."

"I mean if you take it away, what have you left but the law of the jungle, fangs, and claws? If God does not exist, all manner of murder and mayhem are permissible. On a personal scale, if a vigilant Christian deity is merely the product of our desperate imagination, then why comport yourself as a gentleman with an Emily Dickinson?"

"Because I respect her. I respect my wife. I do not wish to spoil my family nor Miss Dickinson's reputation."

"But that assumes goodness and respect and family are intrinsic values. If a gang of marauding Vikings came out of time and landed at Gloucester and marched across the Commonwealth pillaging and raping and arrived at

Arrowhead and cut your head off and dashed your son against a rock and took your Lizzie as booty, what good would your respect and love of family be?"

"What an astonishing thought."

"Such things have happened and happen still and shall continue to happen surely as long as man walks the earth with a club in his hand, and time passes and in the end the lives of the victims, the sounds of their lamentations, mean nothing in the end."

"Like the ants you have just drowned with your urine."

"Precisely."

"And how does your vigilant all-seeing Christian God tolerate such a thing?"

"Rereading Livy's *History of Rome* I was taken, appalled, by the scale of murder and destruction and retribution that was taken for granted in those days and we are talking about the empire and culture that has most influenced and civilized our own!"

"I'm getting lost, Nathaniel. I thought you were making an argument for the existence of a Christian God."

"I am. I do believe in Him. I have to. The alternative is too terrifying. But where do *you* stand?"

"Was Jesus the Son of God, whatever that means, who died for our sins and was he born of a virgin? Is there really a heaven and hell and purgatory? Did Moses actually part the Red Sea, did Christ raise Lazarus from the dead? Did Christ himself return from the dead after his crucifixion and ascend bodily into the heavens? I confess the only saint I have any sympathy for is Doubting Thomas."

"So, you are not a Christian."

"There is not a culture I have read about, studied, or lived amongst that does not have a creation myth and a

roster of deities to back it up and to establish a moral crite-
rion from, to try to explain who we are and where we have
come from. So clearly, to my mind, the religious instinct
is as real as the ones pushing us to hunt or to mate. Everything I see in nature speaks to me of a divine presence, so
in the end, I do consider myself a religious man. To think
or be otherwise would be both arrogant and foolish. But
as for being a Christian, choosing the Christian fable over
all the others merely because of where and to whom I was
born, does seem a bit arbitrary. I had this very same discussion with Austin Dickinson who shares these doubts. Why
must there be a singular, true religion that negates all the
others?"

"Surely they cannot all be true."

"Not in the particular, no, but just as surely they all contain common elements. And that is as far as I have gotten in
meditating upon such transcendental matters my friend. All
this weighty talk makes me thirsty."

Hawthorne ignored this last comment and Melville
wondered whether it was due to the man's level of involve-
ment in the discussion, or embarrassment from having run
out of drink, or perhaps it was just plain New England
stinginess.

"The Bible is a damn fine book," Hawthorne said, thus
increasing Melville's suspicion that the explanation was
one of the latter two.

"I concur."

"The Quran, the Upanishads, they don't come close."

"I disagree with you there. Though I am not an expert,
what I have read of those two texts, in translation of course,
contain passages of great beauty. Good books are written by
good writers."

"But the Bible and the Quran purport to be the word of God, handed down, like the Ten Commandments."

"I think we can agree that to be an exaggeration."

"What the deuces do I know?" He looked away, a weary expression upon his face. "I'd forgotten how dangerous it can be conversing with this heretical side of you."

"Dangerous? Now that is an exaggeration."

"Coaxing me to think of things I'd rather just leave be."

"First of all, it was you who broached the topic to begin with, and second of all you are as heretical as I am, Nathaniel . . ."

Hawthorne laughed while wagging a forefinger back and forth, disavowing the claim.

". . . Oh yes," Melville continued. "It's just that you are better than I at keeping all of these matters separate in your heart and head."

"I've a less volatile temperature than you I suppose. It's like you leap first and only contemplate it afterward."

"Is there anything left to drink?"

"Oh, dear. I am sorry. There must be. Port for sure."

"Just a glass if you don't mind before I ride back home."

Hawthorne left and then almost immediately returned carrying a very polished silver tray with a crystal decanter half filled with port and two matching glasses.

"I must say," he said, pouring them each a measure, "from what you've told me, I do regret having missed making the acquaintance of this Spanish duchess. What did you make of her? I noticed you greeted me today speaking in Spanish. Perhaps it's something in the air."

"'T'was pure coincidence, I assure you."

"Coincidence, the mortal enemy of tale-tellers like ourselves for whom everything is connected in one shape or form."

"Now that is an interesting thought. You are correct. I cannot recall a single time, in anything I have written, that I have chalked up to chance."

"Since Homer, and before him, we like things to fit, to be predestined, to have meaning."

Upon hearing this further elucidation of an insight that possessed implications more profound than even Hawthorne might allow, Melville realized that the duchess and the salutation offered to his friend and small son that afternoon had, in fact, been related. In his barn that morning, during a lull in his writing, the chase of *Moby-Dick* in high dudgeon, he had masturbated himself sending jets of jissom into piled bales of hay. Something in what he had been writing combined with his general state of sexual frustration, one that had only been exacerbated by his recent affections for Emily. To arouse himself he fantasized about her, resorting to his Nukuheva scenario, swimming naked with her, holding her derriere in his hands, invading her relentlessly as she cried out for him. And as this torrid novelette sailed on, charting its own course, the duchess appeared as well, making for a threesome, inducing all manner of Kamasutrian combinations until he was spent.

He had not thought about the woman at all, hardly, and neither had he been unduly attracted to her considerable charms when he met her. Nevertheless, she had emerged from the recesses of his brain, ardent and without explanation, a symbol for him perhaps of wanton womanhood. Later on in the day, and surely because of it, he had spoken with his mother about what she could remember of his father's stories about his travels to Spain. All of this, innocently and inoffensively had led to his choice of language when riding by and surprising Nathaniel and Julian at Love Grove. And from this additional insight, all pondered over in the fewest of seconds, he derived a conclusion. That things were often more related to each other than it might at first appear, so that it was worth the effort to examine what really transpires within one's mind, and, that many crucial things in one's life, and in the life of nature, happen by chance, to a degree of which humans found so frightening that they denied it and made up stories, myths, poetic explanations, religion itself for all he knew, to palliate the underlying terror of it all. He had laden his own tale of *Moby-Dick* with intimations of fate and destiny, describing all of the events in an almost biblical tone, sometimes intentionally, sometimes not. But perhaps The Whale itself was the embodiment of the terror that surrounds us, the darkness we come from and return to, the vast cosmic indifference located on the other side of the sun and moon, the ease with which the sea can swallow us and the wind buffet us, the sadistic certainty of the grave awaiting us despite all of our attempts to breathe and to love.

"She was not one of our Anglo Saxons."

"Well, certainly you would know a thing or two about that. Let's see then . . . dark, curvaceous, masses of black hair, a *peineta* and red leather boots."

"No. She did have a *peineta* in her hair but she was blonde, an unusual golden blonde, with perfect skin neither dark nor white, nor even mocha. It was skin the color of a polished bone, of the best ivory used for scrimshaw—medium height—slender, not curvaceous at all."

"Are you sure she was Spanish?"

"Not only Spanish but from Andalusia, in the south of Spain, from Seville, with an Irish ancestor tossed in. According to Susan Morewood, the girl's family is older and richer than England's royalty, to which she is also related. She wore black, a black dress, black shoes, black stockings, and a magnificent black and white shawl with lots of fringe. Stunningly beautiful and sensuous. Aristocratic and sensuous at the same time."

"Good God. And she threw herself at young Austin you say?"

"She attached herself to him, quickly, if only to keep the other, older and heavier hounds at bay."

"And are you certain you were not howling along with them as well?"

"She was too sure of herself. It made her less attractive to my eyes. And her taking it all for granted that she could have any man in the room made her instantly unappealing to me. But she was still a pleasure to behold."

One of the things he loved about Emily he realized just then, was the astounding mixture of self-confidence and insecurity she presented, blended together in such a way so as to make her irresistible for him. And she read! Like him, not because someone advised her to, not even for self betterment, not so as to acquire more interesting conversation, but out of passion. She was a creature of deep passions housed within a delicate corpus of New England propriety.

"My Sophia has beautiful skin."

Ah, the burgermeister, thought Melville. At first nervously randy on this wifeless evening of bachelor talk, then threatened by the very woman he wished to hear about and fantasize about no doubt, finding her all too much for his provincial tastes, and then retreating into an idealized portrait of his wife. Though Sophia, Melville admitted, was fairer than his Lizzie. He had cast a semi-lustful eye upon her on more than one occasion, something she readily perceived and disliked him for, although he chose to interpret her disdain and displeasure as a sign of vulnerability toward him. But neither of them was the duchess. Neither of them was Faraway. Much more to the point, neither of them was Emily.

The aesthetics of their nakedness, of his and his wife's together, had become problematic over time and would only continue to do so. He saw no way back. This might very well be human nature. It might very well have happened with Emily too if they had been living together these past four years as man and wife surrounded by excessive family. But they had not, and he resisted the idea that such a thing would happen between them even though he had only been with her for a few days. Not all of the chemistry that flows between couples is the same by any means. He had seen and lived this in his own life and observed it over and over again in others. What he felt for Emily was rare and she herself was the rarest creature he had ever encountered.

He had been married to Elizabeth Shaw, his sister's dear friend, since his return from seafaring, and the idea of them being naked together in the light of day was no longer appetizing. It was a terrible thing to admit. He surmised that birthdays tended to steer one into these kinds of dark currents. Trying to look at things objectively, he recalled the Eden they had been banished from as it were, and had to confess it had never seemed that grand a paradise. Back at the very beginning of their courtship, he supposed it had been sufficiently exciting for the both of them. But it had not lasted for long. Their sexual encounters soon took place under the cover of darkness and had remained there where the eyes were censured, allowing the imagination to come to the fore. Since Malcolm's birth, her body had changed significantly, it had begun to resemble his mother's, everything had gotten rounder and thicker. His own physiognomy had not changed that much, but it would. He had noticed that Hawthorne's Sophia had retained her slender frame even after the birth of their third child and she exuded a somewhat mysterious air that lent her an erotic hue. But she was stern too, sterner that Lizzie. Who knew what went on within their bedroom? It was difficult to imagine she and his friend locked in a compromising embrace with any of the intensity or abandon he had felt with Emily, or with the tenderness Lizzie was capable of when she rallied.

He knew, at moments like these, that his relationship with Emily was doomed. He was married and committed to someone else who was about to give birth to their second child and Emily was not the sort of woman to put up with such an arrangement, at least for very long. And the society they lived in was very strict about such matters. Hawthorne was saved from all this *sturm und drang*, older, less impulsive, more fastidious, content to portray his marriage as a continuing love affair in a manner Melville found impossible to emulate.

It was past midnight when he saddled up to leave the Hawthorne property. They were enveloped by the night, surrounded by rolling countryside that had settled into its ripe and verdant pose of summer. Though hard on his friend at times, he realized at moments like these, on the verge of bidding him farewell, how much Hawthorne meant to him. He had no other friends to speak of, no other close friends, and certainly no one who truly understood what his creative life entailed.

"Go slowly," Hawthorne said, reaching up his hand to shake Melville's. "No need to break the neck of a good horse."

"I shall try. And I shall come by again on the sixth, in the chariot, to pick up you and Julian, *n'est-ce pa?*"

"We shall both look forward to it. *Buenas noches.*"

Melville smiled in the dark and touched his hat in the same way he had earlier that afternoon. *"Buenas noches."*

Back out on the main road he hesitated for a moment, battling an impulse to ride all the way to Amherst. It would take him what was left of the night. He wanted to see her. Just seeing her would be enough. Just to watch her from a distance as she came out of the house and took a seat on the Dickinson porch unaware of his presence. Of course, he could invent an excuse to come by and call upon them and surely they would ask him to supper. But they would just as surely detect his feelings. He was not that cold an actor. And what to say to Lizzie and to his mother and sisters who were surely already worried sick about his continued absence at this late hour?

He turned his horse homeward and off they went with just a bit of moon affording them both enough light with which to see the necessary minimum. A riot of stars hung over them, some that went shooting across the heavens whenever he looked aloft. The wonder and the vastness of it and the damp earth smells and the noise of the swaying boughs to either side of the road made of the journey a holy thing.

When he permitted himself to think back upon the night he and Emily spent together, what he most remembered was a brief moment he would treasure for the rest of his days. It did not entail a kiss or anything overtly sexual. After sating themselves without resorting to coitus they had lain there together in the dark, in silence, astonished at what had occurred. And when they recovered speech they conversed in whispers for what seemed like hours until it was he who began to feel overcome by sleep. He turned away from her, almost involuntarily, eyes closed, sinking fast, and then felt one of her little hands upon his back. She rested it there, and then caressed his back, gently exploring and comforting him at the same time. The next thing he knew it was daylight and she was no longer at his side.

Though surely a confluence of chance, it was nevertheless true that two weeks after riding back to Arrowhead that evening, and at the same hour, two other journeys of note took place. María Luisa Benavides y Fernández de Córdoba who had been detained in Manhattan for longer than she had wished, was asleep in her first-class berth aboard Isambard Kingdom Brunel's magnificently refitted *SS Great Britain*, on what would be its final voyage back to London from New York. As the ship passed four leagues south of Montauk, thirty-five miles to the northeast, Fiona Flanagan dropped from the fantail of the steamship ferry *The Empire State* en route to Newport and New York. As María Luisa breathed calmly while dreaming of a garden path at a finca belonging to her family near Palma del Río, Fiona coughed and sputtered but did not cry out before descending into deep cold seawater east of Block Island Sound. Her period was three weeks late, Austin had ceased writing to her and she could not face her family. It was these two events, word of which reached her some ten days later, that gave Emily Dickinson the final excuse she was seeking to overcome her shyness and write a letter to Herman Melville.

13

Amherst

Master Commandant,

Since our return to Massachusetts, I have started and then destroyed numerous missives to you, sir—perhaps this one shall survive and prosper—Father and mother and sister Lavinia so enthusiastically embraced the tale my brother and I were forced to convey that father threatens at least once a week to invite you and Mr. Hawthorne to supper— Imagine how strange a thing that would be!

Our home—always a source of delight for me—seems smaller since the journey—like a remembered dream from childhood—But as the days go by, I have adjusted to it again, and what feels more dreamlike now is all that transpired since you and Mr. Hawthorne came a-calling.

Then, just yesterday, as if to ratify reality's wooden ruler, the sort used by punitive teachers to smack the palms of rebellious students—the bracing reality that puts all flights of fancy to risible shame—word of two concurrent events reached Austin that I feel compelled to share with you, if only to dilute their considerable weight from my own small soul.

I believe I mentioned the young woman my brother felt such a strong inclination for—a colleague and fellow teacher—the Irish lass. It seems she has ended her life in the most lonely and horrific manner imaginable—leaping from the very same steamship you took us upon to New York from Fall River, the town in which this unfortunate creature and her family lived. Austin then received a note written by the Duquesa Mysteriosa, posted just before embarking on a ship heading back to the old continent—it seems both young women were in the same oceanic vicinity on the same evening, one perishing of her own volition far from shore, the other safely asleep under linen covers—or so I imagine it. And I imagine it often, and each time it sends a disagreeable spasm through me. Austin is most changed by it and has put aside all inclinations to be his own man and to strike out on his own and has transformed himself, much to the joy of my progenitors, into his father's faithful heir, a molting I both understand but that, selfishly perhaps, saddens me. At least you, my friend, had, or I should say, grasped, the opportunity to sow your wild oats upon distant shores for a number of years before returning to marriage and family whereas it seems that Austin will only have had our escape to Manhattan.

To think that I, too, was at sea—not only on the massive steamer—but in that minuscule skiff as well! All I can say is that it was your company and presence in both instances that calmed all fears and made me feel—in spite of those potentially perilous events—as safe as I do when I stroll to our First Congregational Church each Sunday.

And there you have it—I do feel better now and for that I thank you as well.

I hope and trust all is well with your beloved spouse and family.

Your friend, E

Pittsfield

Dear Emily,

It was a delight to receive your letter on this day, although I am saddened to learn of the Irish girl's untimely death. For those of us who have lived extensively at sea, death by drowning, whether it be self-inflicted or accidental, is much talked about and seen. Though difficult to imagine, there is a general consensus amongst mariners that, as final moments go, drowning has its merits—the lore stating that, once the struggle ceases, great peace fills the body and spirit before it departs this Earth.

As long as I am dwelling on this gloomy theme—and it was not at all the manner in which I had envisioned writing my first letter to you— I must confess to another death of sorts that saddens me as well. Generally it is me who collects the mail here at Arrowhead, driving my horse

*and carriage into town at a pace that frightens any of the
women folk from accompanying me, and though the contents of your letter to me are beyond reproach, I deem it best
that this correspondence remain private, and I only hope
my replies to you reach your eyes only. If you could assure
me of such a thing, I will rest easier. It is for this reason,
following a Hindu funeral ritual as it was described to me
by an old harpooner far more widely traveled than I, that
after reading your letter various times, I proceeded to my
own "Shmashana" by the bank of a nearby stream and con-
ducted a cremation.*

*Your description of the affects these recent events have
had upon your brother is of great interest to me. I have a
tale I intend to work on, once The Whale has been put to
rest, that would chronicle the evolution of a young man's
passage through the storms one inevitably encounters. The
last time I saw Austin, he had the appearance of someone
who had already ceded to the inclination to withdraw to
harbor. The gaiety and gameness displayed throughout the
first few days we spent together had abandoned him. Clearly
his encounter with the Siren of Seville had, for reasons we
shall perhaps never learn, primed him with solemnity. Then
to receive such news so soon afterward must indeed have
been extremely difficult to bear.*

*Being the oldest son, or, as in this case, the only son
as well, is never easy, even with the privileges of pri-
mogeniture. Though it pains me to say so, I sometimes
wonder—to myself only—if my life would have been more
conflictive and confusing had my father not passed away
when I was still a young man. It was always upon my oldest
brother Ganesvoort where the heaviest burdens and pressures*

fell and it took a terrible toll, so terrible that I truly feel it brought about his most unfortunate and cruel death—at which point the "title" passed on to me!

All this being said and though I hold your brother in high esteem, it is your own well being and state of mind that most concerns, interests, and compels me—and on this account you have been customarily unforthcoming.

The picnic with Nathaniel and his son and the Morewoods and the Duyckinck brothers, all of whom you have met and charmed, was a mighty romp of Berkshirean exploration and a great success. The only thing lacking was your company, an absence I felt throughout and with an oftentimes acute intensity.

Now it is the next day and early in the morning. The household is still abed and I am here at my grandfather's desk that I long ago placed in the unused barn and upon which rests my manuscript to which I must now return.

H.

Amherst

Capitaine Armand de la Mer Pacifique,

The postman in this busy house is Austin who, despite his recent armistice with the venerable values of the Amherst and Dickinson world views, deftly handed me your letter with a friendly wink. Lest I draw too much from his co-conspirator's ocular twitch, he immediately counseled me in his older brother fashion to "be careful." I assured him I would while doing my best to appear sufficiently grave

*and then proceeded directly to the privacy of my room to
read your news.*

*Although Christian by birth and conviction and thus
under no obligation—and in fact prohibited from the
observation of any Hindu rites—I nevertheless concur
with your modus operandi and have obtained a box of
phosphorus sticks. But it pains me greatly.*

*Perhaps you omitted further details of the Berkshire
excursion because you had already tired of describing it
for other correspondents, or because your writing day was
upon you—so I shall have to suffice with the abbreviated
crumbs tossed my way. There is one particular you failed
to mention. I wonder if Elizabeth, your spouse, was able
to join you in her current state? Because of the closeness I
feel to you I think about her—the heat of the season—
the weight of the child—the allergies you mentioned that
she is prone to. Please do not circumvent the topic for my
sake.*

*My room is oppressively warm and still. The sky is
heavy. A powerful rain would be the thing to cut through
it. One yearns for summer all winter and then for the
arrival of autumn on afternoons like this.*

I think often of our Cardinal's Deck.

E.

Arrowhead / Pittsfield

Dear Emily,

Elizabeth is a fine woman and a loving mother and a wise wife to her husband. For many if not all of the reasons you enumerated, she was unable to accompany us on the Berkshire Excursion.

Men away at sea for extended periods of time react in different ways to the deprivation of female society. Crude brutes react crudely—men of more hidden persuasions, like those of our escaped slave and our New York poet, react with indifference, although most pretend otherwise for appearance's sake—gentlemen, a loose category, loose enough so as to permit me to include myself within it, react in a generally gentlemanly manner, with patience and forbearance, two qualities tested mightily when the ship puts in at a port where temptations—some of them risky to one's physical and moral health—often abound. Despite my exotic and well-documented interlude upon and around the Marquesas Islands and Peru, the duration of which can seem greatly exaggerated due to their having been chronicled in my first published books—the vast majority of the time I spent far away from our shores, was spent at sea in the exclusive company of other men. When I returned to New England, to Boston, and for reasons too complicated to enumerate here, I was forced to remain aboard ship for a number of months. Being at sea, surrounded by miles of open ocean on all sides for weeks on end is trying enough—but being legally compelled to remain on a ship when only a gangway separates it from cultivated society, is more akin to being a prisoner.

To wit . . . When I was finally discharged from sea duty and allowed to walk among men and women immersed in what might be called civilization, I was especially disposed to embrace that sector of society I had been sequestered from for such a lengthy span of time. During my absence, my dear sister Helen had befriended Lizzie Shaw. They had each paid numerous visits to the other's household and had become much like sisters. The Shaws are from Boston, and it was to their salon and dining table that I was most generously invited upon setting foot on the mainland.

I suppose that what I am doing here is an attempt to explain how it was I came to be engaged and then married. In the end, for all of the seafaring, whaling, and South Sea adventure, it may be a tale similar to many a man's. It has been my observation that people, in general, rarely stray far from home and encounter their mate nearby, often embellishing a next-door neighbor with unique qualities perhaps more appropriate to 14th-century novels of chivalry. All in all I have been fortunate, for I have seen other couples less suited to each other's temperaments having to forge ahead under the yoke of society's demands. I cannot claim to be that miserable, and in the household where we live I am a virtual king, a ragged one, but still the sovereign.

But, like my father and my brother, like all men, I shall die someday, perhaps sooner than later, Lizzie too, everyone here in my house, all of my children, and everyone in your house—including you. We are alive now, breathing now, and I am in love with you. I love my wife and my family. But I am not in love with them. I am in love with you. It is not a reflection of any moral weakness on anyone's part —it is merely a fact—a fact of Nature not to be denied—thwarted perhaps—thwarted almost for sure—but there it is, like the dried dove dung stuck to the edge of this writing desk—like the watercress thriving in the cold little stream nearby—like the child whose heart beats within Lizzie's womb.

H.

Amherst

King and Sovereign,

What is it, I ask myself, about you—even as you waste ink explaining things that require no explanation, declaring yourself the contented chieftain of your tribe—that even then I enjoy reading the words? I would like to think it so because of my feelings for you, but perhaps it is merely due to your well-known talent for writing. Furthermore, after reading this last letter, I ask myself as well whether these highly exalted sensations we claim are not just another example of the pedestrian embellishments you refer to. Given our mutual penchant for words and literature, it may be that the icing we fashion upon our humble cake is more elaborate and baroque than those of our neighbors, but made from the same "common" ingredients.

Far be it from me to claim a particular individuality—the elements shared between me and the rest of womanhood far outweigh minor and few distinguishing traits. And of these I fear I shall someday be known more for eccentricity than for any lasting merit—and—as you point out repeatedly—what lasts at all really? Our phys-ical selves least, a poem, a book, a sonata, longer, but what good does that afford the deceased creator?

You make a bold assertion, a declaration worthy of Lancelot himself. But the wedded Guinevere here is you my captain, and I am incapable of doing battle with that. Thwarted, of course, it shall be—and victory, not even a Pyrrhic one, impossible. And as we both know, it is I who stands the most to lose. To Kings are allowed all manner of foibles and peccadilloes, whereas for paramours, once discovered, there is only banishment and humiliation.

My natural disposition tends toward seclusion. Even here in this too-populated house, I endeavor to keep to myself all that I can. If I possess a genius for anything, it is for looking at all things small and drawing from them large conclusions. Tis a skill that enables me to stay put without going mad. The excursion to New York and back required of me an inhuman leap of faith, a radical, one-time departure from my normal sedentary self. I cannot conceive of doing anything like it again. The very notion of leaving the perimeters of Amherst, of our own front yard, dizzies me into vertigo. But what a glorious exception it was—one rife with treasure I shall examine for as long as I continue to breathe the sweet air of Massachusetts. And the knowledge that you, too, are inhaling the very same ether just a swallow's flight away is more than I require.

E.

Arrowhead

Emily,

What have I done to upset you? What torpid male stumbling have I committed to vex you so? I have said too much of myself. I appear all consumed with myself. It is as if I walk about—swagger perhaps being a better word—with a full-length looking glass attached to me so that I might admire every triumph and tragedy at every moment, every act of kindness, noble thought, and every indiscretion, making of it all the most engrossing spectacle on earth. I am an actor playing to an audience of one using other beings that surround me, yourself included, as opportunities for expanding my performances to their best advantage. The whole thing is ludicrous and despicable.

Well, I crack that looking glass here and now. I take a harpoon and a hammer to it and smash it into bits, ripping off its cumbersome harness, ignoring all of the bad luck incurred through its shattering.

No more of my exploits and vanities disguised as deep thoughts. Thanks be to the gods this book I am finishing leaves me out of it. I look back upon all the others preceding it now with acute embarrassment—pages and pages of badly masqueraded braggadocio.

You must wage war upon your tendency to seclude yourself. The young woman I was with and knew riding in the stage to Boston, sailing to New York, charming the salons and oyster bars of Manhattan, acting as first mate on our nautical adventure from Orient Point—the beautiful, independent, vivacious, intelligent, well-read, and compassionate woman I knew upon a New London evening must not to a nunnery remove herself.

Might I at least be the one who aided and encouraged you to open your life rather than narrow it down.

From this point forward, I pledge strict avoidance of all Armando pomposities.

One important simple truth—I have never had a better time, felt so alive, felt such a fever of attraction to anyone, than the time I spent with you. At least upon your return to Amherst you have regained a situation of solace and comfort. Since my return to Arrowhead my life feels bleached. I go through the motions but my heart and spirit are not in it. Luckily thus far only the dog notices. And so I abandon myself to Moby-Dick. All of this said mind you without a single glance toward a looking glass!

H.

Amherst

Master Melville,

It is I, not your first but hopefully your second mate, who must beg your pardon today. It was a bad moment at a bad time for me to have written you my last letter. Though I must say it was possibly worth it for having provoked the image you conjured—of yourself tethered to a looking glass! I laughed aloud upon picturing it and caused my parents considerable concern at supper today when, without any visible reason, I burst out laughing again in the midst of our meal. At least this did not occur during our daily family prayer service!

And speaking of bad times, I must consult you—you in your role as a man of the world.

Austin, understandably, continues to mourn the loss of Fiona and thinks about the suicide in a most repetitive and alarming manner I do hope you are correct regarding the merciful side to death by drowning—Last night he confessed to me his gravest fear—that the young girl's motive for such a drastic decision may have had to do with a pregnancy. It seems such a thing was possible between them. My question to you is—and I am embarrassed to display such an ignorance—but I cannot go to my mother with such a question and Lavinia is younger than I—I can assure you I am familiar with the basics on this theme—it is only with some of the details that I suffer certain lacunae.Would it have been possible in your estimation for Fiona to have known if, in fact, she was with child after only a period of some three weeks since their last "meeting'?

At the moment, he mourns not only the woman who so filled his spirit with Spring in a way I fear his betrothed shall never do—but a lost child as well. In private with me, he speaks of little else—tormenting himself with the image of mother and child, sodden and bestilled, washing up upon some gray and stony strand along the coast of Rhode Island. If there was an argument I might employ to rid him of the smallest of these two ghosts it might help him recover with more alacrity.

As I have been writing this, I have watched a small spider at my window making a bad decision to spin a web in a corner, starting from the lowermost sash of the window that is raised a foot or so from the sill—for tonight I shall have to shut it closed and long before then the girl who cleans our rooms will have swept the creature's hard-won handiwork aside without a second thought. Plucking

*with my fingers the single initiating silken strand the lit-
tle creature started with and hung from, I leaned my arm
out the window and let it drop. Surely it survived the fall
without a scratch and hopefully it was not pecked at by
some vile bird and now, at least, it can begin anew at some
more fortuitous spot about the foundations of our house.
And I wonder if there is a lesson here . . . before starting
a great work, any great endeavor, including a romance,
one must do all one can to choose the best "place" to begin!*

E.

Arrowhead

Dear Emily,

*With my looking glass contraption now destroyed and
without reviewing the whole sad story that got me to
where I am today, suffice it to say I chose the wrong "spot"
from which to spin my web and here I am stuck in the
middle of it!*

*On the other hand, perhaps the lesson to be learned
from your spider's fable is that we all start from where we
can, some with more luck and success than others. When it
is time to spin, it is time to spin, and spin we do—affixing
that first strand to the nearest mooring cleat. Oh, that
your much-missed fingers had been present four years ago
to alter the "spot" from which I have woven my web.*

*I am no physician—but having lived my life sur-
rounded by womanhood and having been privy to many
and all details concerning the female reproductive cycle,
I can offer the following commentary about your brother's*

dilemma. Do we know for certain that their last "meeting" took place three weeks prior to the suicide? Might there have been an earlier liaison? I seem to remember your mentioning that they had worked together in Boston at the same school. If, in fact, it was just three weeks that passed between their last meeting and her death, and if at the moment of their coupling she was at the very end of her fertile days and if her monthly effusions arrived with chronometric precision, then it would be possible that she concluded—but far too soon and rashly—that she was with child. Many "ifs"—too many for me. The cycles of some women are remarkably precise, especially in young women, but for many it is inconsistent and highly variable and subject, I have been told, to mental angst. The fear the girl surely had of being pregnant may have been the primary cause of a delay in her cycle. I wish I could tell you more or provide you with some ironclad conclusion. The one certain thing you can emphasize with your brother is that there is no way she could have been even close to certainty regarding a possible pregnancy. At least a month's delay would have been necessary to reach such a preliminary diagnosis.

Time will heal his wounds.

And thinking of time and of wounds, I wonder whether this is the beginning of a long and felicitous correspondence or an attempt to hold on to something precious and lost for as long as we can. I try to live my domestic life as best I can, giving all their proper due and working diligently to finish The Whale. But what I live for, are these letters. And, of course, I think—it is only normal that someday your affections toward me will alter, undergo a transformation, and affix themselves more properly to someone else—someone freer and with no need to be hidden from view, someone who can be at your side. The mere thought of such a normal and inevitable occurrence fills me with dread. Dearest, dearest Second Mate—my queen and princess, my inspiration, my north star, my morning tide. . .

H.

Amherst

Mon Cher Armand,

Less than one month ago, my life was calm, predictable, tedious at times, but virtuous. Since you dismounted in front of our house, filling up our salon with your singular concoction of city sophistication, maritime exoticism and wilderness wisdom, standing beside your august, more familiar and less dangerous friend—I find myself enmeshed in scandal. Some of it my own making (!) I implore you thus to not condemn me further by implicating me as a "spot" from where, had you known, you would have spun your web four years ago—when I was only sixteen!

I have conveyed your most suspiciously knowledgeable opinions concerning Fiona to Austin as if they had been my own and it did seem to placate his anxious state considerably. I thank you for that and only hope I can someday repay you.

Now—not only are you a man, with all such a condition implies, but you are an especially vigorous, out-

going, and impetuous example of the species—armed, thank goodness, with a pen or, once upon a time, with a harpoon aimed at sea monsters rather than with a spear or club—and thus you are susceptible to fits of jealousy, suspicion, and despair. The force of your spirit frightens me and incites me at the same time. Thus it was from the first moments when I met you until we bade each other farewell.

Do you truly fear my feelings for you are capable of so rapid a cooling? Do you think someone like me meets and then relinquishes her heart to someone like you very often? Do you have any real idea who I am or of how I am or from where I am? (I write these lines with a smile, not a scowl.) First of all, the odds that any swain my parents would approve of, not to mention myself, for I am far more particular still, will approach our door at any time in the future are small indeed. I would like to think of myself as so much a prize to be fought over but I am not that woman. And even if such a gent were to materialize and win my hand and inspire trust enough for me to marry— I know how this gent would be—and he would not be anything like my Master Commandant. This position in my heart that you have invaded and possess is not subject to further pillage and is not subject to the wear and tear of time, dear man. You have done me in and all that is left for others to claim, were that ever to happen, is a shell, one that will wrinkle and darken over the years while my blood now incensed forever with my master's fire, will course on like one of your raging ocean storms.

E.

Arrowhead

Dearest Emily,

Do you really exist? Have I not conjured you into my brain for solace in this universe ruled by despots and krakens? Are you not some figment of my far too romantic imagination brought forth like Venus from her shell to sweeten a life surrounded by meals and visitors, a peevish wife, an intrusive mother, and a bevy of unmarried sisters? I take my little Malcolm and my massive hound on long walks during the afternoons and I take you with us. The summer clings to the land with a sad desperation closing its eyes and ears when the night breeze arrives bearing a telltale chill that rattles the leaves with a sound all too characteristic of another season. Each day the water of the lake is colder and more invigorating. You will be pleased to know I have taught you to swim and you dart about around my son and I like a shameless Merrow.

I have news. On this final day of August, spurred on by the added disruption my father-in-law's impending visit to nearby Lenox to preside over trials, an annual peregrination requiring my household's utmost attention and condition of vassal-dom, and amplified this year with the feature of his daughter's pregnancy fast approaching its conclusion—after cloistering myself away in the barn this entire past week—I have finished this morning The Whale.

I penned in the final period, thought of you, gave it to Augusta to copy out, and went out for a very long walk, alone, physically alone but otherwise accompanied by your spirit. The sensation of peace and contentment that invaded my heart was only tempered by the regret I feel at not being able to dedicate The Whale to you. When a copy finally has the good fortune to drop into your hands, you will find it dedicated to NH (I plan to surprise him with it). But know, dear girl, that it is really meant for you.

H.

Amherst

Master,

I am so touched, so transformed, so proud of my Captain. Swell the wave, ripple the tide, vast and deep the under-tow.

E.

Amherst

Armando,

Contemplating your dedication and remembering one of the first conversations that took place between the four of us here, in this salon, where I sit this morning blissfully alone—I thought something like this might be appropri-ate for you: In token of my admiration for his genius, this book is inscribed to Nathaniel Hawthorne.

E.

Dear Emily,

The words you suggest for me are more than perfect and thus shall it read, and the fact that they have come from you means the utmost to me. The final proofs went off today to Mr. Craighead in New York, the only change being the title—for I have decided to name the book more specifically after its main protagonist.

Fetching today's post my disappointment at not finding anything from you—you must forgive my greed—was somewhat relieved by an agreeable surprise in the form of a letter from none other than our William Johnson. As I opened it I feared it might contain trouble of some sort, but then I was quickly set right reading the man's inimitable god-fearing prose.

Quite aside from the joy I felt in perusing its contents was the far greater joy, one not unmixed with melancholy, I experienced as remembrances of the time we spent together flooded through me. It all came back in a great rush of images and sensations that I confess brought me to tears.

I cannot write more today, but I shall here conclude by faithfully transcribing a passage from William you will, I am sure, appreciate:

In this distinguished home in where I work, a teacher comes every morning after chores to give me and the cook lessons in all manner of erudition. We all are treated well under this roof. I was just going to write "under this mas-

ter's roof"! But Mr. Wheeler, a merchant who buys and sells grains and lumber and slabs of granite, makes a point of telling all of those In his employ that we is equal and the same as he under the grace of God Almighty. I know that last part may not mean much to you, sir, but perhaps you might pass this along to Miss Emily, who I know shall understand. The Lord works in mysterious ways, sir—— that's all I know——I lay down before him and accept what travails and joys he see fit to send my way. I am certain, sir, that over time, Miss Emily will show you the way—— that her good nature will find and take hold of yours and bring it unto the light whose brightness and sweet warmth shall clean your doubts and resistances away. I received a letter from Mr. Whitman——a proper one asking me proper questions as to my progress here——but as an exercise of faith and holy resolution, I shall not reply and I do hope he will understand. Perhaps, sir, you could tell him for me and say that I ask for him to strive as well to find and stay upon the Lord's righteous and narrow path.

Amherst

Dear Mr. Melville,

What great relief and satisfaction it gave me to read William's words. I thank you for passing them along. It does sound like he is doing well, an outcome that was never guaranteed, and so I am thankful for that as well. And yes, I can hear him as I read him, and I am tempted to write to him and say that if he ever tires of his current duties he should consider coming to take over the church here in Amherst. The sermons given by our local pastor, regardless of their proper grammar and judicious choice of scripture, are painfully dull. When I read William and remember his very particular cadences of speech, I am drawn to return to the fold with the same eager spirit and depth of faith and conviction I had years back, before I was exposed to and corrupted by your satanic excesses.

Father and mother are off to Boston next Tuesday for a few days. Austin improves and spends most of his free time with his betrothed, Miss Susan Gilbert, with whom I am getting along very well. The two of them parade about like a couple already long married. So it will just be Lavinia and I here to keep the household running—a turn of events that I hope will also give me more time with which to write to you.

When do you think a copy of your Moby-Dick might be available for a provincial soul like mine to read?

E.

Arrowhead

Dear Emily,

I beg of you—do not respond to this letter with an answer, but rather with your appearance. I will be there regardless, next Wednesday, by eleven in the morning, and shall wait for you until sundown if need be. I would prefer to wait in vain all day than to receive a negative response from you earlier by post. If you are unwilling or unable—so be it. But if you could find a way . . .

Where—you ask?

Upon reading of the trip your parents are making to Boston, I have contacted a friend who keeps a hunting cabin well hidden along Lake Warner, near Stockbridge and Hadley. We could spend the day there alone together. So, I propose we meet at the cemetery in North Hadley.

H.

14

Nel mezzo del cammin di nostra vita
mi ritrovai per una selva oscura,
ché la diritta via era smarrita.

— Durante degli Alighieri

In New England, there comes a day each September, usually toward the end of the month, when autumn first asserts itself. Regardless of how much sun is shining or how green one's land and trees remain, a breeze arrives announcing the banquet's end. Though resistant to precise description, one nevertheless knows the minute it appears, unlocking sentiments at once familiar and melancholy. For one's heart takes note—one's heart senses the kingdom of finitude exerting its forceful dominion—instilling in one regret for all the bounty taken for granted and that is slip-ping through one's fingers, regret at time's inexorable vec-tor, regret at youth's heedless penchant for merry squander.

The breeze arrived at Amherst and Pittsfield, Massachusetts, early on the morning of the twenty-second, as Emily dressed for breakfast and as Melville saddled his horse. Both were too distracted to give the announcement its full due, even as its effects took hold of their spirits.

As Melville rode to Hinsdale and then on to Worthing-ton and Chesterfield, and from there to Haydenville and Hatfield, the breeze and its effects dissipated as the sun rose spreading heat through clear air. At Hatfield, he took a second breakfast and then rode north to catch a small rope ferry across the Connecticut River when clouds began to drift in from the East. By the time he reached the cemetery at North Hadley the sky was shrouded in gray and the morning's breeze was back threatening to cast a pall upon the day.

Melville tied the reins that fell from his bridle about a birch tree, one of many that ran along a perimeter of the churchyard, leaving his weary horse to graze. He walked slowly between verdant rows of gravesites, resigned to spend the entire day there if necessary. The older tomb-stones went back as far as 1790. Each one stood above a plot of earth where a coffin had been lowered and covered over and in each coffin the remains of a dead human being. He saw families buried together. He saw the headstones of children and of women who had died giving birth to chil-dren. Some of the oldest graves held the bones and uniforms of veterans who, like both of his grandfathers, had fought in the War for Independence. For a moment the thought crossed his mind of Elizabeth and the difficulties she was having with this second child now so close to entering the world. If something were to happen to her his way to Emily would suddenly be clear. Such was the degree of shame that filled him for ceding to this macabre fantasy that he almost returned home.

But it was just then he saw the horse and carriage. It had come to a halt not far from his horse. Emily, dressed in white, held the reins and was seated next to another young woman he presumed to be her sister. For a brief second he was nervous, almost to the point of losing heart about the whole assignation, wishing he had never put it into motion, almost preferring the epistolary realm their relationship had evolved into—to this sudden return to flesh and sinew. As he drew nearer to them and observed her more clearly, the shy warm smile upon her face and the anxious smile upon her sister's younger and wider visage, his hesitations and second thoughts fell away from him.

"Good morning," he said to the both of them.

"Good morning" Emily said with a brave and somewhat forced cheerfulness. "Mr. Melville, I present you my sister, Lavinia."

He offered the young girl a curt bow. "How do you do?"

"Very well, thank you, sir."

"How was your journey?" Emily asked him.

"Long. I had to leave before dawn. But very beautiful too."

He went up to his horse and untied the reins. "Do you think you might follow me for a bit? Just a few minutes, down to where the canoe is kept."

"Surely," said Emily. "Lead the way."

The small caravan made its way onto a grassy road that went gently downhill passing through a narrow stretch of forest before bisecting a pasture so bright with sunlight—due to a sudden parting of the clouds—all three of them had to shade their eyes.

"So," Emily said to Lavinia, "how do you find him?"

Lavinia looked down at their feet trying to repress a grin. "Old. I find him scandalously old."

"Old? He is only thirty-two, and just."

"He is handsome."

"Yes, he is."

"And very married, Emily."

"We have been through this."

"I know. I just cannot get over the shock of it. And now, seeing him, I feel like an accomplice to a dangerous crime."

"I will not go over all of this again."

Melville could not hear them and only looked back a few times with an encouraging smile as they neared the lake. What most occupied his mind were the palpable facts of his current reality. That Emily was there with him, there riding just behind him and only a few minutes away from the beginning of a day they would spend together without any intrusion. Though tempted by nature and character to look ahead toward the day's end and to go on and consider the odds of their being one day found out, he threw up a wall against it. The lake at that spot was largely obscured by another growth of trees. The water, normally crystalline, was at that moment muted and somber from additional low-laying clouds moving in above them. The trail narrowed where the stand of trees began, but the wagon made it through and, coming out behind Melville into another smaller clearing, the lake was suddenly there, calm and majestic and pristine. At the end of a small wooden dock built out from the shore, was an overturned Indian canoe.

Melville dismounted and gave his horse some oats from a feedbag tied to his saddle and then tied the reins over a branch of a sturdy pine making sure the horse would have shade in case the weather cleared. Then he unfastened the saddlebag and draped it over his shoulder and made his way over to Emily's side of the wagon.

"There now." He raised a hand to Emily. "Let me help you down."

Such was the sensation that seized them when their fingers touched as she alighted from the wagon, they barely heard Lavinia's meekly intoned question. "At what time should I return?"

"Shall we say around six p.m.?" he replied. "I do hope this is not a great inconvenience for you, Lavinia."

She looked down.

"Not at all," Emily said, answering for her sister. "Vinnie has a good friend in Hadley she has arranged to spend the day with, and we are all sworn to secrecy upon the threat of a long and cruel death."

"There will be no need for that I'm sure," Melville said, looking directly at Lavinia with genuine sympathy.

"Six o'clock it is then," The younger girl said, still not looking at him.

"I am very grateful," Melville said.

And then she did look at him, briefly, without saying anything, but offering a quick little smile. He thought of commending her to have a good day, to be careful, of announcing he would take good care of her sister, but none of it seemed appropriate and all of it felt awkward and it was with relief that he watched the girl turn the wagon round with an expert's pair of hands, saying nothing further, either to him or to her sister. Together, side by side, they watched the wagon go back through the trees until it broke out onto the pasture again and began to make its way up the incline at a brisk pace owing to Lavinia's use of a whip.

He reached for her hand.

"Emily. I do not quite believe it."

"Nor I."

"How have you managed it?"

"I told everyone the truth—that I was to pass the day with a friend."

"Surely they asked for more details that that—Elizabeth and my mother certainly did."

"Yes. It's true."

He turned to face her and took her in his arms. She pushed into him and closed her eyes and took in the smell and the feel of him, surrendering, shame and gratitude mixing. "Where is it you are taking me, Captain Bluebeard?"

"Bluebeard was a murderer. I am only a poor kidnapper, and a short-term one at that."

"Then lead me to your pirate's cove before we are discovered."

"Right this way."

They walked to the end of the dock and he squatted down by the canoe, turning it over. The paddle was there. He put it aside and then carefully put the canoe into the water.

"Do you really expect me to travel in that?"

"I do."

"Is it safe?"

"It is with me at the helm. It is not the most comfortable craft and you will have to sit very still, but the journey is not long and I expect you will enjoy it. Come."

With one hand he held the canoe fast against the end of the dock and with the other he guided Emily onto the forward seat, a flattened spar. Then he grabbed the paddle and his saddlebag and sat down on the rear seat and used the paddle to shove off and away.

The truth was that many years had passed since he had last commandeered a canoe and it had been a much larger one than this back when he had spent his time in the South Pacific. But he took to it right off and took pleasure in moving them into the middle of the lake. The wide blade of the paddle moved through the water smoothly, providing the light craft with impressive propulsion. She sat as instructed, very still and very straight and it was a source of delight for him staring at her back and posture and at the graceful way she moved her head to take in the view and to turn and speak to him. But after a few minutes, the leaves of the trees along the shore turned over and the water's surface began to ripple from a characteristic breeze and rain began to fall.

"What a nuisance," he said, "and of all the days."

"I suppose," she said, "but the truth is I don't mind it at all."

She raised her face up to the lowering clouds, closing her eyes, meeting the rain coming down that moistened her forehead and cheeks. She smiled, unseen to him, at the thought that each time they met some journey upon water intervened. Looking down to her right at the water she observed fish near the surface, brought up by the rain, swimming along with them, the water a mixture of blue and gray and the Northern Pikes dark brown and spotted on top with silvery speckles underneath.

"Who is your friend—the owner of this cabin?"

Melville prayed for the rain to stop. Though clearly not his fault it felt to him as if it was, as if the fates were already vying to see which one could ruin this day more for him. "He is the son of a wealthy landowner from these parts, a family not unlike mine except for the crucial difference that they knew and know how to make money with their money rather than just spend it all away, a practice my father in his day and his brother to this day and I myself excel at. The fellow introduced himself to me after reading Typee and fancies himself a gentleman naturalist with a great interest in Native Americans. This canoe of his is authentic down to the last detail, and the cabin—I've only been to it once before with him—resembles a small and somewhat ramshackle museum dedicated to local fauna."

"Does he know you are taking me there?"

"Lord, no. He is in Boston and thinks I have come to use it as a hideaway where I can finish my book. The idea gave him great satisfaction."

"And is it terribly far?"

"No." He could see that her dress was drenched with rain about the shoulders. "If my memory serves me correctly we are just a few minutes away—up around the next bend. I'm so sorry about the rain."

"Don't be. I am most thoroughly enjoying it, and besides, too much sunshine can be a bore."

Her words relaxed him and filled him with a degree of admiration that excited him. What manner of woman was this? He recognized that comparisons were odious but he could not help but stack her up—she who at first glance seemed so delicate and in need of pampering, only to demonstrate time and again a character much the opposite—

against his spouse and sisters. Emily seemed to possess an adventuresome spirit kept quietly simmering within an encasement of decorum and drawing room, Puritan civility. He wondered to what extent she was unique. Might this surprising blend of qualities be generational? Perhaps there existed a vast number of young American women in their twenties out there still dressing and serving tea like their mothers, but filled with wanderlust and grit. But he doubted it—or if such a trend was there—it was not yet developed to this extent. What he saw in his own younger sisters and nieces, what he saw in cities and towns told him otherwise, told him that conformity still reigned supreme, conformity made duller still by an air of self satisfaction that so often engulfed it.

Pleased he had remembered the terrain correctly he saw the cabin as they pulled around the bend. Some fifty yards ahead and toward the right great boulders rose up out of the water extending onto shore and on the other side of them he could make out the narrow beach and in the woods just up from it partly hidden by birch and pine, the two-story wooden retreat.

"There it is."

It was raining steadily now and the two of them were soaking wet. Unlike Melville, Emily was in no hurry for the canoe ride to end. She knew it was impossible to get soaked any further and thus the damage—*sans importance*—was already done—whereas the sensation of mystery she was feeling from this adventure, so out of her ordinary—making their way in the rain to what would be their sanctuary— was intensely pleasurable. She placed her hands at either side of the canoe and leaned slightly forward, studying the little house in the woods. Then she looked to the side and back a bit, not focusing on Melville as much as on the paddle he was pulling through the water. She made a point of memorizing its flat blade of blond wood and how it gleamed under the water's surface, making its own little eddy, and she memorized the curved wooden sprats that strengthened the delicate hull. She dipped her right hand into the water and was surprised to find it warmer than she had expected.

"There is no dock or landing, I'm afraid, so I am going to have to run us onto the sand as best I can." And he thought—what was I thinking bringing her here? This is a place that, selfishly, works for me, and the dear girl is doing her best to not be difficult or to show her disappointment, but what a terrible and inconsiderate blunder. He had envisioned the day, all during the past week, with sunshine.

He rammed the canoe as deep into the sand as he could, but even so, Emily had to put her shoe into a bit of water stepping out. She made as if she did not notice and Melville, seeing everything and further appalled, attempted to mask his misery with activity. He jumped out of the canoe, water up to the midcalf of his riding boots, slinging the saddlebag back over his shoulder, and then he shoved the much lighter craft further up onto the beach.

"Go stand on the porch, Emily, before you catch pneumonia. I will only be a minute."

She turned and did as she was told and he cursed the rain gods for their cynical cruelty. He pulled the canoe up to the very edge of the narrow beach, as far from the lake as possible, then turned it over and stuck the paddle underneath it.

Emily was shaking from the chill spreading through her and from nerves. She watched him wrestle with the narrow Indian boat. She could not imagine seeing her father, nor her brother, nor even Mr. Hawthorne ever doing such a thing. She realized she had never seen any of them do anything remotely physical apart, perhaps, from saddling a horse. Melville, she recalled, fed his cows. Melville sailed ships and sloops and boats. Melville chopped wood and had harpooned whales at sea. She found his physicality, and the grace with which he exercised it, healthy and masculine, unaffected. Even upon occasion when he might seem to do something impulsive or rough, it did not deter her admiration. Compared to the prevailing gentleman's code that left manual work and any tiring activity to underlings his style seemed to her a paragon of what in her romantic imagination it meant to be American. Even when she pictured him writing in that barn he had often described to her in his letters, the image she formed always took on an energetic tremor.

He joined her on the porch, found the key in its appointed spot and opened the front door.

"I will light us a fire straight away."

To his great relief no field mice or raccoons darted out the opened door. The cabin's interior was reasonably neat and well cared for. A stuffed fox lurked upon the mantle above the hearth. Two Navaho Indian rugs ran parallel to each other in front of the fireplace stepped on by two comfortable chairs. A fine table with straight-back chairs was placed near the rudimentary kitchen. There was a slight musty smell in the house that, with the rain, was not unpleasant. He lay the saddlebag upon the table and took off his coat, draping it over the back of a chair. "I've brought some food and drink. Lets find some blankets and I will build a fire to dry our clothing."

Too agitated to stop moving about, he went back outside and piled up dried splits of beech and oak from the woodshed, flicking away beetles and spiders. Emily climbed the narrow stairs and found a rustic but charming boudoir. A brass bed with a quilted coverlet, a chest of drawers, even a mirror, and a small bookshelf well populated with a peculiar mixture of beautifully bound classics—Ovid, Dante, Homer, Aeschylus, Herodotus, Marcus Aurelius—and leather-bound oddities devoted to trout fishing in Scotland, the early tribes of North America, the seals of Antarctica, an introduction to Algonquin grammar. One blanket was folded at the foot of the bed and she found another in the chest of drawers. Quickly she undressed down to her camisole and petticoat, wrapped one of the blankets around her and then regarded herself in the mirror. Her hair was a mess, a damp auburn swirl of rain induced curls she detested. But she had only her fingers with which to try to attend to it and she quickly abandoned the endeavor with a small moan of frustration. Going back downstairs—carrying her clothing and shoes and the other blanket—she found Melville in his shirtsleeves feeding an impressive blaze. Some of the wood cracked and the smell of singed bark and evaporating dampness along with the heat emanating from the stone hearth was comforting and cozy.

"Well done," she said.

He turned and looked at her, rising to help her with the blanket and her shoes, admiring her spunk yet again for having disrobed so matter of factly. He pulled a wooden chair from the table up near the fire for her to arrange her dress over.

She freed a bare arm from the blanket around her while making sure to keep herself decent. The slightness of her, forgotten since their last encounter in New London, provoked him even as he found it endearing. They sat in front of the fire, in silence at first, until Emily took the situation in hand.

"I have but one wish today, an infantile one."

"And what is that?"

"That we might stay here forever."

He thought perhaps she was going to say something else, that she wished the weather had been better, that they had met upon another day, in another place, that they had never met at all. He took her hand in both of his.

"Emily."

"I know it is not fair, to you, to your family, to my family. Thus its infantilism. But I wish it fervently. Can I not do that for just a moment?"

"Of course you can."

"It is a sweet little house you have brought me to on a lake long part of my world. I could clean it and make it snug and hospitable for us. You could work, and catch us fish, and we would only see other people when we wanted to, in very small doses."

"I had forgotten, in my way, the why and the how and the extent of my feelings toward you."

"You should be ashamed."

"Ashamed I am. Perhaps it is a writer's curse. After the four days we spent together, weeks went by and until today the physical you, the real you, has been supplanted by a literary version locked within the confines of my head."

"And was she very dull this literary me?"

He laughed. "Not in the least. But she was my creation and subject to the limitations of my stunted imagination."

"Am I so different from how you remembered?"

"Yes. The real you is far more original, far more stimulating. I felt shy at first when I saw you with your sister. Then it all came rushing back."

"When you took my hand."

"Yes. You felt it then too."

"At the very same moment."

Then her smile faded and a wistful expression took its place.

"I realize this has to be difficult for you. Perhaps seeing each other again was not the wisest decision."

"You cannot mean that."

"I am thinking of you."

"It was I who suggested and planned it."

"And I who acceded without a second thought."

"Is that true?"

"Almost."

"It is difficult for you as well."

"But less so. I hide my feelings from Austin and my parents, from Lavinia until the other day. But I have no further commitments, no one else lays claim to my affections. My 'loneliness' is not without its advantages. I have no cause for regret."

"Never have I understood so well the meaning of that word," he said.

She gazed into the fire and then looked at him. Her hair was still damp, one of her shoulders, gamine and smooth, was bare, exposing the thin white cotton strap of her camisole. Her dark eyes glistened and her lips were partly open. He kissed her. He grabbed both her shoulders, turning her to him as the blanket fell away and continued to kiss her. When her tongue entered into his mouth he felt himself invincible. Overwhelmed he drew away from her and kissed her forehead, the sides of her face, the back of her neck.

"Emily."

She put her arms around him, embraced him and, looking away, spoke in a whispery tone, "What are we to do?"

"We will be fine."

"Are you certain? I leave it to you. I was better until I saw you again today, and now I fear I shall be lost without you, and I do not understand it."

An hour later, the sun was out and a tide of fresh air entered in through the bedroom windows. Melville was asleep and Emily leaned up on her elbow to look at her man. His mouth was slightly open and he made an occasional snoring noise. His shoulders were broad and muscular, the hair on his chest slight and dark. His manhood rested in a gentle arc between his legs. Regardless of what the future would bring, this was the man fate and then her own will and appetite had chosen—and she was pleased.

She rose from the bed taking care not to wake him. Of the fire only fragments of wood remained transformed into glowing embers. She opened the door and let herself out onto the porch. After looking and listening in all directions and satisfied there was no one else about she proceeded down to the shore, walking carefully upon the path. She had never been naked outdoors before and found its novelty exhilarating. Once free of the trees, the sun shone down upon her body, warming her with a clarity and freshness particular to September. She passed the overturned canoe and stepped upon the sand and waded into the water and kneeled down.

She had read a digression in a botany text at the Amherst library that described how some species of animals and birds mated for life. The human species was not mentioned. But that, she supposed, was what the scriptures were for. She realized too, and not without a smile, that she on that day was living proof Melville was not among the faithful. But perhaps she was.

She admitted the possibility that, owing to her youth such a radical conclusion might come to her more easily than when she was older. Perhaps she would want children someday with the sort of man her father approved of. But she considered this possibility there very briefly, as a nod toward objectivity, a gesture whose real purpose was to bolster the sensation captivating her at that moment. She could not imagine wanting to be with anyone else, could not imagine sharing such a degree of intimacy with another body and spirit distinct from his. She could identify with the gray wolf and the pen. He would return to his home and family and, for all she knew, perhaps sail off again to some distant corner of the globe to revel with yet another gam of native women. She did not care. What she cared about was how his large life had intersected with her little one.

Melville awakened and saw her, Emily as water nymph, from the bedroom window. As he took the blanket she had used and wrapped it around himself and hastened down the stairs to join her, he too sensed with a pointed certainty that he had found the woman of his life. But he had found her too late. This thin and nervous girl, raised on his own soil with her singular mind, who could never be his. Her young body he had just possessed that played before him naked in the water, something his own wife would never, ever willingly do, would remain elusive. He had married and had his children too soon, and now it was too late. Perhaps it had been necessary, he thought, opening the door and going outside, for him to go through all that he had, including his marriage to Elizabeth, in order to have reached this place, in order to have attained this appreciation for Emily that so cruelly overwhelmed him then. Why, he asked himself, why was life so often like this?

Determined to put it out of his mind, to not pollute the hours left to them that day, he ran the rest of the way down to the narrow beach, howling like a madman, causing her to turn and smile at his adolescent antic, as he cast off the blanket and ran into the water, diving down under it as soon as it was deep enough. He swam out, taking deep, aggressive strokes. She watched him with just the sort of adoration he hoped for. You have been so far away, she thought, a stranger, a man, and I your latest conquest. May God not permit me to conceive this day—or I shall die—I shall join Fiona without a second thought.

He swam about, cleansing his spirit and attempting to empty his mind, and then swam back to her, standing and walking toward her. He fought an urge to cover himself concerned he might appear shameful or foolish and so he quickened his pace and sat down next to where she had moved, seated on the sand with her feet still resting in the small lapping waves. He leaned over and kissed her.

"You see what power love has?" he asked.

"Which is that?"

"It has driven the rain and clouds away and brought the sun back to us."

"Is it love that did all that?"

"What else?"

"Passion perhaps . . ."

"That too. They go hand in hand."

"Not always."

"No. Not always. But in this instance, absolutely."

"Are you so sure?"

"Very. Why? Are you not?"

Her knees were raised and she leaned forward and rested her chin between them. The little knots of her vertebra stood

out under her pale skin. She had only meant to tease. The repartee had begun in a spirit of jest. But something shifted. For reasons she would never be able to satisfactorily explain, his question irked her.

"You cried, upstairs," he went on, hoping to clear this sudden shoal.

"Yes."

"Did I hurt you?"

"No. At first a trifle, then quite the contrary."

"Were your tears then just from passion?"

"Having never done such a thing before, I would not know."

Coral dug into his hull. He felt ashamed, thrown off the pedestal so recently erected to celebrate the wiser, older man.

"It was only the thought," she said, "that this is what happens. This is what throbs beneath the nave of that baroque cathedral of worry, ritual, and prohibition—this tender, violent, animal thing."

"Animals we are."

"You've often said so."

"Have I?"

"Yes, and I agree." Why, she wondered, was he vexing her so?

He thought perhaps he should have stayed swimming out in the lake longer. "I do love you, Emily. I have never felt like this."

"Nor I."

"So there."

And there, she thought, was where the discussion should be left. But she was unable to do so. "And do you not love your wife as well?"

He paused.

"You know I do."

She tossed a stone into the water

"Then what is this we have between us?"

"This is different."

She threw another stone. "Why?"

"I have tried to explain all of this to you in my letters."

She paused as well and wished to be back upstairs with him just as he rolled off of her, but something pushed hard, pushed back, within her.

"It is almost autumn. The leaves awaken drier each morning. Squirrels harvest acorns to store. Birds contemplate their southern journeys. Sap slows within all of these trees. And you, as you so often insist, are an animal too, a heathen in Christian garb who has lived with cannibals and their concubines."

"Please, do not turn me into a caricature, not that one at least. I have fallen in love with you."

"You barely know me—really."

"I know you more than you think. I had hoped and even assumed, perhaps foolishly, that to be evident by now."

A breeze blew suddenly across the water, sending ripples along its surface. It caused their skin to chill.

"Your wife is about to have your second child. She is in a foul temper, as well she might be, and you are frustrated by it, and there I was teetering to fall for Mr. Hawthorne's Buccaneering friend. I think I prefer to view all of this as passion and discovery. I can live with that—understand that. Love is too complicated—for me, a hank of yarn all a-tangle. We have no future and well you know it."

How was it possible, he thought, to go from such joy to such dread in so short a time? "Why are you doing this?" he asked. "Why are you saying these things? We have been honest with each other from the start. I am not a complete fool, a complete animal. I have lived long enough to know that regardless of whatever "future" we may or may not have, I am in love with you, heathen or not, in my own heart. Perhaps it is only passion for you."

His last words went out across the lake. They sat there as the afternoon deepened and as the waning sun reddened their upper backs, their bare feet in the clean water, their genitals tight, the dense woods and rocky shore on the lake's other side reflected with a tender clarity. A fish jumped and startled her and she began to cry. She leaned into him, and he put his arm around her, and kissed the top of her head.

"Forgive me," she said.

"I hope you can forgive me."

They did not eat the food he brought and both felt too affected from their conversation to make love again. Emily dressed upstairs and stripped the bed while Melville tidied the hearth. She tied her shoes and did her best to straighten the stiff wrinkles in her dress and to fix her hair. On an impulse she took a miniature copy of Dante's *Inferno*, published in the original, slipping it into her purse before going downstairs.

He paddled them back. The sun had descended behind the western forest, but still hovered unseen above the horizon, casting a denser, richer light upon the entire landscape they were part of. Dining needles and gnats flew in erratic swirls over the water, and fish rose to feed. All that had been rained upon and blown about was purified and dry again and still. It was as if the whole late afternoon had dedicated itself to a final celebration of the dying season.

Emily sat facing him. Over his shoulder she watched the cabin disappear behind the bend. Just as she had feared hours earlier during their arrival in the downpour when Melville had been so irritated, the blissful grace of that approach was now a thing of the past, replaced by the penance of departure. She imagined the little house still there, quiet again, its walls and furnishings rid of their presences. The fox above the hearth, the brass knobs atop the bedposts, the chair backs where their clothing had dried, the mirror she had looked upon, the books in that dusty shelf, all but one, closed, their pages so filled with history and wisdom pressed against each other in a darkness that might last for years. That place where they had loved and argued, caressed and been alone with each other would someday burn down or simply fall into disuse, eaten up by nature and neglect. Perhaps the room at the inn in Connecticut would last longer, but it too would someday be replaced with something else as the decades went by. Nothing lasted. There was some comfort in that for her. Time would smooth all of life's current furrows into a seamless story. The worries and burdens that had impinged upon them, that had threatened to wear them down as a bull is diminished by the overweight picador, would be lost and forgotten as the years wore on. This she knew and treasured. The happiness she had known that day, that he had given her, would stay with her. All the rest was but another squall. Tears returned to her eyes, just as Melville saw the dock coming into view behind her.

"Herman," she said, smiling at him. He looked at her, calmly resigned to bear whatever it was she wished to proclaim. Given her state it was difficult for her to get the words out. She looked down, composing herself, and looked up at him, speaking in a hoarse whisper, "I love you so that I fear I shall break."

He lay the paddle down letting the canoe carry on by itself, and reached out to her with both hands, and she took them into her own.

15

One month later to the day, Stanwix Gansevoort Melville was born. Elizabeth suffered tearing during the delivery that required stitching and though she was able to nurse the baby from her right side, her left nipple became occluded, engorging the breast. She traversed numerous episodes of great pain for a number of weeks and Melville was mired in guilt because of it—guilt from his hidden transgressions and guilt from the extent to which his romantic affections had been conferred upon another. The latter state was one he had no control over, but it did not interfere with the compassion he experienced and the devotion he paid to his wife. He did all that was within his power to help her. Well attended, thanks to the bevy of capable women in the house, she encouraged him to continue work on his new project and to get out and about.

He swam each day in the lake even as the temperatures dropped. He chopped wood daily, organized and took active part in the apple harvest, orchestrated the cider pressing, and spent the early mornings working on the new manuscript.

Since the day spent with Emily at Lake Warner, not an hour went by he when he did not recall it in great detail, regretting many moments but treasuring many more. What most tortured and consumed him was the extent to which he schemed and wracked his brain to try to bring about a second rendezvous. On a number of occasions, when immersed in a plot for seeing her again that might succeed, imagining how that might be, giving free rein to fantasies in which neither of them had further cause for worry or restraint, he would hear the new baby cry, or, worse, hear his wife cry out in pain. His reveries, oftentimes lascivious, would evaporate into the cold air as he plunged himself into a cauldron of self-loathing. And Emily did not cooperate, did not reciprocate or show anything but a minimal amount of understanding or empathy toward his repeated complaints. Once news reached her of the new boy's arrival, he noted a distinct alteration in the general tone of her letters that arrived less often. It was as if she had decided to take all that had passed between them into the inner sanctum of her room where she might protect it.

Thus it was that when word arrived from New York announcing a definitive publication date for *Moby-Dick,* he grabbed hold of it as if it were a Kisbie Ring. On November 11, he took possession of four copies. Before leaving the post office he penned a note in one of them for Emily and sent it straight off to her. Then on Friday, November 14, he drove his wagon over to the Hawthornes and invited Nathaniel to supper at the Curtis Hotel in Lenox. Sophia, still nursing Rose and busy preparing for their move away from the Berkshires, was glad to get her husband out of the house. Melville timed it in such a way so that the meal would commence later than was usual. By the time their last course was dispensed with, they had the hotel's dining room to themselves.

"I feel compelled to say again how very saddened I am to see you leave the area."

Hawthorne lit up a cigar, taking his time.

"We shall not be all that far away, and we can strike up a grand correspondence. Sophia and I will be sad to lose your company too, and Julian, but I, for one, look forward to leaving Lenox."

"How so?"

"Have you not noticed the people gawking at us since we arrived, and how they are now gaping in from the bar?"

"Really? No. I haven't."

He looked about and did indeed quickly see red and whiskered faces, some with pipes, some with their mouths open, staring at them.

"This is the first time they have seen me in the village in the two years I have lived here, and they are wondering why. I have fame as a recluse and a snob—you, too."

"Me? Nobody knows me here."

"Some do—Sophia tells me all the local gossip. But it is I they are most perturbed by, I who live so nearby in a house owned by one of the local elite, I who have never attended a single church service or any public celebration since my arrival."

In the adjacent bar and sitting room, the locals were, in fact, talking of little else. What might it be that has drawn the elusive Hawthorne to town today, to dine like this in public view with the even more eccentric recluse from Pittsfield? What might they be plotting? How long have they known each other? Is this, perhaps, their first introduction? Why would the distinguished author who has never paid the village any mind, come to supper with Melville, known for little more than his dangerous wagon driving habits, his odd dress, and the fact that his uncle Thomas spent so many months imprisoned for debt in the local jail? Those more in the know were perplexed because the older author, who dressed like a real gentleman, was famous for his dark Puritan tales while the other, who sometimes resembled a scarecrow, was known for books rumored to invite their readers to licentiousness.

"I wanted to thank you for sending *A Wonder Book* over to Malcolm. He will be very touched when he is old enough to appreciate it, and I was very moved for him."

"He is going to be a fine boy. And now you've another. We must take good care of our sons, Herman. You and I, who lost our fathers at so young an age, know that better than most. They are our great gifts to the world, far more so than anything we might write. But there was no need to invite me to this extravagant meal for such a thing."

"I thought we should meet and celebrate our friendship one more time before you and Sophia depart—and I have another motive as well."

Hawthorne raised an eyebrow. His cigar had gone out and Melville leaned forward with a candle to help him relight it.

"I've a book for you as well."

"No."

Melville smiled. "Yes." And then he leaned down and removed a copy of *Moby-Dick* from his satchel that rested on the floor near his chair.

"At last."

"At last. It is being published in New York this very day." He handed it to him. "And I wanted you to see the dedication before anyone else did."

Putting his cigar down, Hawthorne took the volume in his hands and then put on his spectacles. He moved his plate aside to make room for the book, opened it at the middle and stuck his nose deep into the pages for a good smell. Then he went to the beginning and found the words dedicated to him that Emily had composed. Underneath Melville had written his name, the place and the date in ink. Hawthorne read it over a few times and then closed the book, hesitating before looking up.

"I do not know what to say."

"Are you pleased?"

"I am more than pleased. No one has ever dedicated a book to me before, Herman—and what a book it is. It is I, now, who am profoundly touched. You shouldn't have— there being Lizzie, or your mother, your children, your late brother or father."

"All of them worthy in their own way I suppose, but none more than you. I do not use the word genius lightly."

He thought of Emily as he spoke, the sole person in all the world he truly had wanted to inscribe it to. "And though I do love and did love all you just mentioned, none were writers, capable of understanding what it is we do, none had the heft to guide me through this book like you.'"

"I did very little."

"You may genuinely think so. But I know better."

By the time Melville dropped Hawthorne back at the little red house for the last time, the air was cold and the day's light fast diminishing. All in all it had been a grand and special day. The leisurely manner in which they had eaten their meal and the modest amounts of alcohol imbibed sat well within him as gathering clouds and a dropping temperature cleared his head.

The book would be all over New York on the morrow and at last his myriad debts would be repaid, paving the way for a far better life for he and his family. As he coaxed his horses to pull the wagon along that lonely country road in deep New England with no one, not even a fox about, an anonymous man returning home, he sensed that fame would soon embrace him and that he would have to resist its clutches with steadfast guile. Lizzie would improve. The new boy would grow. Malcolm would cease being called Barney as he inched his way toward the adventure of adolescence. His mother would remain the great smooth keel keeping their frigate afloat with the wind behind them. His sisters would marry. The new book he had started would further solidify his place in the emerging world of American letters. And he and Emily would find a way.

Surely, he would find a way for them, starting, it just occurred to him, with a journey back to Europe. He envisioned a book tour through England and France, through Italy and Spain that he would invite Emily and Austin to accompany him on. Perhaps the Whitman fellow could join them as well. Surely, a way would be found to tie it fast, to plot a course that would convince her family and his own of the little group's impeccable propriety. As snowflakes began to fall upon him, he imagined he and Emily strolling in spring along the Seine, imagined them waking together in a modest but well-appointed palazzo astride a Venetian canal, imagined them walking through Andalusian hills awash in olive trees, embracing each other upon plowed red earth with a noble, white-washed finca belonging to the duquesa barely in view.

As autumn deepened that evening, giving way to another Berkshire winter beginning to take hold, it is perhaps as good a place as any to leave him—content in the frigid twilight, under the season's first snowfall, heading back to the hearths of Arrowhead, thirty-two, in love, and on the verge of literary fulfillment. Life itself will take care of the rest, doing what it does, to him and to all, paying little heed to storytellers.

So, let us end our tale here and place a final period below, preserving this version of that now distant time. Biographers and literary critics can write down their own gleanings. No need here to push on and chronicle the humiliating failure that *Moby-Dick* shall be for him. No need to take us through the searing Civil War approaching, or the terrible deaths he shall have to bear—his mother's, Malcolm's suicide, Stanwix's after a long illness, and then the demise of his secret love in Amherst. I will not paint the old age that came his way and then his own death one September, back in the city, not four blocks from where he was born. Many of his last days, to Lizzie's bewilderment, were spent seated upon a park bench in Union Square contemplating The Everett House. Of all the possibilities that ran through his excited brain that evening as the wagon wheels creaked and spun atop the snowy route home, one that never occurred to him was the leaden fact that he would never again set eyes upon Emily Dickinson.

Paris, Madrid, Corrubedo